A HOME FOR SU-LAN

1—H.F.S.

A Home for Su-lan

by
Margaret Rossiter Thiele

PACIFIC PRESS PUBLISHING ASSOCIATION
Mountain View, California
Omaha, Nebraska   Oshawa, Ontario

CONTENTS

Outside the Wall

It would soon be time to go home, but Su-lan did not want to go home. She would put it off as long as possible. She was cold, but it would be cold at home, and dark as well. Here above the moat pigeons dipped and turned under the blue, blue sky; bright winter sunshine glistened on the silvery ice while the iceboats with sails spread to the wind skimmed back and forth under the shadow of the great city wall.

Su-lan watched the iceboats crowded with merrymakers bundled in their fur-lined robes. If only she had a fur-lined jacket! She looked down at her jacket—a mass of tatters.

Trying to tuck her bare hands into the ragged jacket sleeves, Su-lan ran with the other children and slid on the ice, her long black braid streaming out behind her like a ribbon in the wind.

Every afternoon she came to the moat to play with the hordes of other children who lived in the crowded, crumbling mud huts of the small settlement outside the north wall of Peking.

When her mother protested that it was too cold to be outside, Su-lan would answer, "But I like the fresh, cold wind." How could her mother and the sisters and little brother sit all day in the tiny dark room, huddled over the charcoal stove?

Out at the moat there were so many interesting things to see and do. She could almost forget how hungry she was all the time. And then, sometimes she found bits of food thrown from the iceboats or dropped from vendors' wheelbarrows.

She turned from watching the iceboats and the merrymakers.

"Come, Ai-lien," Su-lan called to one of the girls. "Let's go up and look over the wall."

Together they ran up the steep ramp which led to the top of the wall that encircled the great sprawling city of Peking. This was not just a little garden wall like the ones which enclosed the homes of the people. "This is the highest and strongest wall in the world," Su-lan often boasted to Ai-lien. A giant tower reached into the sky above the huge arch of the gate beneath. Higher and higher the girls went until they were all out of breath.

The girls looked out from one of the windows of the tower. They looked down into the compounds of the people who lived just inside the wall. They could see people moving about, children playing, dogs, chickens, and pigs. Then they looked at the wide, straight street leading away from the gate beneath them, and the traffic moving swiftly along—rickshas and carts, and carriages drawn by horses.

"Oh, look, Su-lan! There is a wedding procession coming down the street. See those banners and the coolies with the green robes. And there is the bride's chair way in the back." Ai-lien pointed. "Surely this is our lucky day."

For a moment Su-lan forgot her ragged clothes and cold hands. She pictured herself dressed in embroidered silks, riding in the flowery sedan chair borne on the shoulders of eight bearers to a new home with clean-swept courtyards and newly made quilts and pleasant rooms with fresh clean paper on the windows.

Su-lan sighed when the wedding procession passed out of sight. Then she and Ai-lien left the tower and walked for a while along the top of the wall on the wide street between the two balustrades. The girls stopped now and again to look down on the moat and the place where they had been playing.

The other children were still playing on the ice. How far away and how small they looked!

"I wonder what is happening over there." Su-lan pointed. "They are all running over to the bank. See!"

"It's those people getting out of the rickshas." Ai-lien giggled. "How funny they look! Oh, I've never seen anyone dressed like that before. Come on. Let's go down."

Away they went down the ramp to join the crowd which was growing larger every minute, around the two strangers. The girls wiggled and pushed their way into the crowd. Finally Su-lan managed to elbow her way into the front line.

"Who are they?" she asked a boy near her.

"Can't you see, stupid one? They are foreign devils."

Su-lan stared at the two persons dressed much alike in short colorful jackets and narrow straight trousers. Both had wool caps and gloves.

"Can you tell if they are men or women?" Su-lan persisted.

"The little one is a woman, I think. But how ugly she is with that yellow hair and those pale blue eyes!"

Su-lan couldn't decide whether she was ugly or not. She had never seen anyone with such pale skin and eyes. Certainly the features of these foreign devils looked strange. Instead of the small, delicate, even features of the Chinese, theirs were larger and more prominent. Su-lan noticed especially the face of the man. Why, his nose looked like a beak, high and long and sharp.

In spite of all this there was nothing terrifying about him, she decided. If he is a devil, he must be a very good-humored one.

The man looked at the children and smiled. Then, turning to the woman, he said something in words the children could not understand. He stooped and helped the woman put on some strange-looking shoes with shiny blades on the bottom. The children crowded closer for a better look at the strange-looking shoes.

"Chu-ba." The man motioned the children to stand back. When the shoes were laced up and the last knot tied, he pulled the woman to her feet. He pushed the children away, and then the woman skimmed across the ice like a bird flying out of a cage—almost as fast as an iceboat in the wind. Su-lan, Ai-lien, and the other children ran after her, but she had gone far down the moat. They turned and saw that the man had put on his own strange-looking shoes and had stood up.

Su-lan expected to see him disappear down the moat after the woman, but his movements were nothing like the graceful swing of the girl's. He wobbled and tottered and jerked along. The children gathered around him immediately. Then he sprawled on the ice, and like puppies at play the youngsters, laughing and shouting, piled on top of him.

"Bu-hao! Bu-hao! [Bad! Bad!]" he said sternly, shaking them off.

"Oh, he speaks Chinese," someone shouted. And they all called back at him, "Bu-hao! Bu-hao!"

The man got to his feet slowly.

"Let's help him," Su-lan suggested.

They surrounded him and propelled him along like a sled.

Soon he made short sallies by himself quite successfully, leaving his helpers behind. Then he turned back to them and said in Chinese, *"Hao-bu-hao?* [Good! Not good?]"

And the children joined in a laughing chorus, *"Hao! Hao!"*

After a while the woman skated back to them. She talked to the man, and they both laughed. Then she tried to help him.

The children shouted, *"Hao! Hao!"* as they watched her skim smoothly and swiftly back and forth over the ice.

At last the foreigners seemed to have had enough. They started to take off their skates. By this time more children had gathered and the crowd had swelled into a small multitude. Everyone wanted to be in the inner circle. Each one started to push and to crowd in for a better position. The space around the foreigners got smaller and smaller. Everyone wanted to have a look at their wool socks and leather shoes. The children's elbowing and pushing changed to punching and quarreling and name-calling.

It was then that Su-lan saw the foreign devil stand straight and tall. He had his shoes on now and he held his skates in his hand. He looked stern.

"Look, children—" He spoke in a language Su-lan and the other children could not understand, but it was not hard to guess what he meant. Su-lan watched every movement. He put his hand in his pocket and she heard the clinking of coins. Then he pulled out a fistful of coppers.

"Now, scram!" he said, and scattered the coppers across the ice.

The crowd broke up at once. Everyone scrambled for the money. Su-lan, strong and quick, darted here and there between the feet and the pushing small bodies. When the scrimmage ended, she held four big pieces of money in her tightly closed fist. Each big coin worth two small pennies! Never had she owned so much money before.

When she looked around, she saw that the other children had all run away. No doubt each one hoarded his own coins, she thought.

Making sure that no one watched her, Su-lan tore off a little piece of cloth from the inner lining of her jacket. She tied her four coppers tightly in it and placed it inside the cotton wadding of her inner garment.

"I will stop at one of the food stalls and buy something to take home to the family," she decided. But after a moment's thought she gave up that idea. She had never handled so much money before. She hesitated to show up her inexperience in buying, and her lack of knowledge of the price of foods. Su-lan fingered the small lump inside the wadding in her jacket. She enjoyed the possession of the coppers too much to part with them so soon. She would keep them until she could decide what best to buy with them.

Lao Lieh, the vendor, stood beside the tempting display of fruits and candies spread out on his wheelbarrow at the corner of Fried Fish Alley when Su-lan entered the narrow lane on her way home. Usually she passed without allowing herself a glance at the frozen persimmons, candied apples, colored sweets, and other goodies, but this evening she lingered so long looking at all his wares that Lao Lieh came over to her. When Su-lan saw the solemn look on his face as he watched her, she tipped back her head and laughed out loud.

"He must think I might try to slip something into my sleeve," she thought.

Lao Lieh reached out his hand to her at the sound of her laughter. "What are you laughing about, you imp?" He sounded cross, but no matter. She was already running down the lane.

Her steps slowed as she neared the gate in the crumbling street wall behind which her people and a number of other families shared a common courtyard. Although the early winter evening had already set in, the gate had not yet been barred. Su-lan was glad she did not have to call old Ma to come and open the gate for her. Poor as they were, they were not without a man to watch at the door for intruders. Now she went over to the second door on the right of the barren square of packed ground.

Before lifting the mat which hung over the entrance to keep out the cold, Su-lan paused. It was only because she knew nothing else to do, had no other place to go, that she came home to this. Each time she lifted that mat and entered the dark room she felt her wild free spirit trapped in a cage, her dreams of palaces and beauty and color and flowers shut out.

But tonight she reached inside her ragged clothes and touched the hard little lump, her packet of coins. "Tomorrow! Tomorrow I'll decide what to get with them." The thought made her smile. Then she lifted the heavy quilted mat and went in.

Most of the tiny dark room was taken up by the *k'ang*, a built-in platform which served as a bed for the whole family. When Su-lan's eyes became accustomed to the darkness of the room, she saw her mother, a thin, weary woman with lifeless eyes. She saw her five small sisters and baby brother huddled with Mother around the clay stove in which a few coal balls made of coal dust burned, giving off a reddish light. Father, a ricksha puller, had not returned yet.

The children began to clamor as soon as Su-lan entered the room. "Tell us a story! Tell us a story!" they begged.

"Why are you so late? You must be very cold," Mother spoke up in a dull, quiet voice, without a change of expression.

"No, I'm not cold," Su-lan answered. "I've been running. I like the fresh air."

A tiny tin teakettle on top of the stove puffed out a cloud of steam. Su-lan picked up a chipped rice bowl and poured herself a drink of the hot water. As she sipped, she thought, "I know. Tea! I'll buy some tea for Mother tomorrow."

"Don't take all the water," Mother warned as she started to pour another cup. "Father will want a hot drink when he comes in presently. And when this fire burns out there are no more coal balls for today."

The stove belched out gassy fumes into the already stuffy room. The children began to complain that they were hungry, but Su-lan knew that their complaining would do no good. One meal a day was all they could have. They would have to wait until tomorrow.

Father usually ate something before he came home. He would stop at a stand or a vendor's wheelbarrow and buy some food for himself. He had to pull a ricksha all day, and he could not work on one meal only.

Su-lan sighed. Then she went over and sat on the *k'ang* with her sisters and baby brother. If only their *k'ang* was like some she had heard about that had a place for a fire underneath to keep the bed warm at night. When the fire in the clay stove went out, they all climbed up on the broad *k'ang* and huddled together for warmth, pulling over them the patched and mended padded quilts that had seen many years of service.

"Now tell us a story," the little ones urged, knowing it was no use to clamor for food.

Su-lan always kept her ears open when out by the moat or in the marketplace for anything that might amuse or interest the younger ones at home. Now in the cold dark room, she repeated a story she had heard in the summertime when the pleasure barges floated slowly down the moat laden with rich people in silks and satins. She had listened carefully to the hired storyteller who stood in the prow of the boat; his voice carried loud and clear to the little girl as she ran along on shore beside the moat.

The Story of the Seven Sisters

"Once upon a time," Su-lan began, "there was a family which had seven daughters. One day the father went out to gather wood, and came across a nest with seven wild duck eggs. He took them home, but planned to keep them for himself and his wife, and not give any to his children. He was a very selfish man, you see.

"The sisters went to bed, and the father went to bed, and the mother put the eggs on to cook.

"After a while the oldest girl woke up and asked, 'What are you cooking, Mother?'

" 'I am cooking wild duck eggs,' the mother said. 'I will give you one, but you must not tell your sisters.' And so she gave her one.

"Then the second daughter woke up. She asked her mother what she was cooking.

"The mother said, 'I am cooking wild duck eggs. If you will not tell your sisters, I'll give you one.' And so it went. At last the daughters had eaten all the eggs; not one was left.

"When the father awoke in the morning and found out about it, he was very angry. 'Who wants to go to Grandmother's?' he asked. But he had no idea of taking them to their grandmother, but intended to lead his daughters into the mountains and let the wolves eat them up."

At this point in the story the smallest listener spoke up. His voice quavered. *"Ai, yah,* how wicked!"

"And then what happened?" another spoke up.

Su-lan smiled at the children. Of course they knew the story by heart, but she went on.

"Well, the five older sisters suspected their father and wouldn't go with him, but the younger two said, 'We will go with you to Grandmother's.' And so they went off with their father.

"When they reached the mountains, he told them, 'Wait here. I will go on into the village ahead and tell your grandmother that you are coming.' He left them there and rode off in a donkey cart.

"The two sisters waited and waited, but their father did not come back. At last they decided that he wasn't ever coming back, that he had left them alone in the mountains. So they went farther and farther into the hills trying to find a place to spend the night. Then they saw a big stone. They thought they could use it for a pillow if they could roll it over by a tree. They pushed and pushed on the stone. When at last they moved it, they saw that the stone had covered the entrance to a cave. A light shone out of the cave.

" 'Now what is this?' the sisters exclaimed, and went into the cave.

"The light they had seen came from many precious stones and jewels of every sort in the cave. There were jars and jars of precious stones and pearls all around.

" 'What a lovely cave this is!' the girls said.

"Then they noticed two golden beds with gold-embroidered covers. 'Let's lie down and rest,' the one girl said to the other.

"So they lay down and slept.

"During the night the owners of the cave came in, a fox and a wolf. They sniffed the air.

" 'I smell human flesh,' the wolf said.

" 'Oh, nonsense. There are no human beings who can enter our cave. The stone covers it up too well for that.'

" 'Very well,' the wolf said, 'let's lie down in our beds and sleep.'

"But the fox suggested, 'Let's curl up in the kettles on the hearth. They still hold a little warmth from the fire.'

"So the wolf and the fox curled up in the kettles, one in the kettle of gold, and the other in the kettle of silver.

"In the morning when the girls awoke they saw the wolf and the fox curled up in the kettles. They were frightened. Quickly they put the covers on the kettles and heaped a number of stones on them. Then they made a fire.

"The wolf and the fox soon woke up. 'Oh! how nice and warm it is this morning in our kettles,' they said.

"But soon it got too hot for them. Then they peeked out from under the lids and saw that the two girls had made a fire under the kettles.

" 'Let us out! Let us out! We'll give you lots of precious stones and gold and silver and we'll do you no harm,' the wolf and the fox cried out.

"But the girls would not listen to them. They kept on making a bigger fire. So that was the end of the wolf and the fox." Su-lan paused.

"Did they cook the wolf and the fox?" one of the children asked.

"No, they just burned them up," another one said.

"I wish we were in a nice warm kettle," another piped up.

"Is that the end of the story?" asked a fourth.

"No," said Su-lan. "Be still and listen."

"The sisters lived happily in the cave for a number of days. But their father was sorry for what he had done, and turned back to look for them. He went into the mountains just where they had gone, and came to the stone. He sat on it to rest. He took out his pipe and knocked it on the stone to empty it of ashes.

"The girls inside the cave heard the knock and called out, 'Who is knocking on our door?'

" 'Are those my daughters' voices?' the father asked. He jumped up and looked around.

"And the girls said, 'Is that not our father's voice?'

"Then they pushed the stone away, and saw their father standing close by. Their father was glad to see them once more. He was much surprised to think that they had chanced on this cave full of precious stones. Then the daughters told him the whole story.

"Their father fetched people to help him carry home the jewels. And when they got home, the mother wondered where he had found all these treasures. So the father and the daughters told her everything, and they became a very wealthy family and lived happily to the end of their days." Su-lan finished the story and looked at the children under the ragged quilt. The youngest had gone to sleep. The others were almost asleep.

"That was a nice story, only I don't like that father," Ming-li, one of the older girls, spoke up.

"Why not?" Su-lan asked.

"Oh, he was mean to try to lead his children to the wolves. I wouldn't have let him into the cave when he came back if I had been one of the daughters."

"I don't like the father either," Su-lan agreed, settling down under the ragged quilt with Ming-li and the others.

In the Dark

Usually Su-lan fell asleep quickly, her arms tight around "Little Six," her baby brother. But this evening she stayed awake thinking about the strangers she had seen, the two foreign devils who threw away money with the sweep of the hand. But mostly she thought about the small fortune tucked away inside her rags.

Four coppers or eight pennies! That would buy a small piece of meat to put in with the millet and salt vegetables; or it would buy a *jin* of white rice—a special treat. Su-lan moistened her lips with her tongue as she thought about the food. But then she sighed. If she bought the meat, she couldn't buy the rice. And what about the tea? How her mother had wished for tea! Surely some of it must go for tea. Yes, she would spend four pennies on tea. How she would like some of the persimmons and tangerines Lao Lieh carried on his wheelbarrow! Oh, my! she felt hungry right now. Well, if she hadn't found those pieces of steamed bread that dropped off the vendor's wheelbarrow in one of the alleys she would have been hungrier, she thought. And then the idea came. "I'll go shopping inside the walls tomorrow," she exclaimed almost out loud. Then she lay back and stared up at the mat ceiling while she thought of the wide streets and many shops and food stalls. She had never ventured into the city. She had only looked down on it from the tower and the wall. But now that she had money she would really go.

Su-lan smiled. The idea pleased her. Then, having decided what she would do, she closed her eyes, and soon would have gone to sleep had she not heard low voices from the other end of the *k'ang*. She hadn't heard her father come home, but it was his voice she heard. Now her mother spoke. Then she heard her name mentioned. From the tone of the voices she knew her father and mother were having an argument. Father's voice rose a little. And then, fully awake, Su-lan almost stopped breathing so she could catch every word.

"But I told you, she will really be better off. And so will we. There are too many mouths to feed."

The voice trailed off, and then her sister, Ming-li, coughed; and the coughing swallowed up Mother's reply. Su-lan listened with both ears now. She heard the names Fan Tai Tai and Ts'ai Shih K'ou. "Ts'ai Shih K'ou! That is the market in the South City. But what about Fan Tai Tai [madam]? Who is she?" Su-lan wondered.

Then father spoke again. "With five dollars we can have heat and food until the end of the Great Cold."

"What kind of woman is Fan Tai Tai?" This time Su-lan heard her mother plainly.

"What an idle question!" Father replied. "What difference does it make? I didn't see her, of course. She will not starve the girl if she wants to get any work out of her."

What could they be talking about? And then the words began to make sense. Why, they must be planning to sell her to someone named Fan Tai Tai. She could hardly believe it. Five dollars! Five dollars was an immense sum of money, of course. She couldn't remember when her father had ever had that much money all at once. It would bring food and warmth to the little ones. Times had been so hard, and the winter was not yet half over. But to be sold, to be traded for money as if she were a horse or—or a cow! Her cheeks burned with shame and bitterness.

She could not sleep now. A choking, burning sensation came over her, and her throat filled with a lump which could not be swallowed down.

Thoughts tumbled about in her mind. True, she had not received any great love or affection from her family. They were not given to expressing their feelings. Life had been a matter of hand-to-mouth existence with little energy left over for good times or fun. Still she had been fond of her brother and sisters, especially of "Little Six."

Maybe she should run away as soon as it was light in the morning. She remembered the money. That would be a help. But still, where could she go? She must save face somehow. The worst thing in the world that could happen to anyone would be to lose face.

If she ran away, her father would not get the five dollars to buy food for the little ones and coal for the fire. After all, she was older and stronger, and she had learned a lot of things about taking care of herself.

Maybe she could save face by pretending she did not care, that she was glad to go. Perhaps she was the lucky one to be able to go.

What would Fan Tai Tai be like, and what would she make her do? Su-lan was strong and healthy, and had a young courage which convinced her that she could work hard enough to please anyone. Possibly the house of Fan Tai Tai might be more pleasant than living in this crowded dark room. Possibly the home to which she would go might be a home of wealth and comfort, where the life of a slave might be better than the way she lived now.

Su-lan allowed herself to dream of a happy future. She began to picture all the details from the arrival of Madam Fan to get her to the time when she proved herself in the new household and was treated like one of the family. She remembered the story of the seven sisters. Maybe she would find treasure in the new home, treasure that she could bring home and share with the family. With her father too? No, she decided firmly, not with her father. She could not forgive her father.

One thing she decided firmly. No one in the family would know that she cared at all to leave them. And so, thinking these thoughts, Su-lan dozed off to sleep.

Fan Tai Tai

When Su-lan awoke, it was hardly light enough to see. But even at noon the room with its grimy, paper-covered window was never very light. She sat up and looked around. The other children still slept. Mother sat on the *k'ang* near the charcoal fire that was burning in the clay stove. "No doubt Father has already gone," Su-lan thought as she slid off the bed and picked up the empty water bucket. She pushed aside the mat door covering and went out into the chill gray morning. If only her family could afford to have water delivered to their home as some of the rich folk did. Already coolies struggled up the rutted lane from the public well, their wheelbarrows groaning and creaking. The water from the full water-buckets sloshing over the sides of the wheelbarrows formed icicles a foot long.

One of the coolies at the well reached for Su-lan's bucket. He fillled it from the overflowing canister that he had just drawn up. She smiled her thanks, as she reached for the bucket, and then started back up the lane, taking care not to splash the water on her legs.

As she walked back to the family room, she wondered if she had really heard her father and mother talking on the *k'ang* last night. By daylight it seemed such an unlikely thing. Perhaps she had dreamed it all.

At home again Su-lan helped her mother with the household chores. She tried her best to tidy up the dingy room and to help keep peace among the smaller children.

Father returned in time to eat with the family at noon. And Su-lan waited for some word or gesture about last night's conversation. But her father ate as usual, holding his bowl close to his mouth, eyes down, not looking at anyone and talking little. She studied him guardedly, more than she had ever done before. It struck her that she did not really know her father; she had seen little of him, for he worked long hours away from home. He seldom spoke to her. And when he looked at her, he did not seem to see her but to be looking through her and beyond. Deep lines furrowed his face. Certainly her father was not much to look at, the child thought.

Finally he finished his meal, put down his bowl and chopsticks, belched politely, and rose from his stool.

"I guess I must have dreamed it." Su-lan sighed with relief, holding Little Six close to her.

Her father shuffled toward the mat at the doorway. Then he stopped and turned. "Tell her to come," he said to the mother.

So, it had come. Su-lan looked at the floor. "Now is the time," she thought. She waited for her mother to speak, but she said nothing.

"Su-lan—" Father turned toward her. "You are coming with me today. I will give you a ride in the ricksha into the city. You will see many new sights."

"Me! Me! Take me! Can't I go too?" the other children began to clamor.

"Silence!" Father raised his hand. "No, only Su-lan." He paused and looked straight at her, and added, "Isn't there something else that she can wear? People may wonder, seeing her in my carriage."

Mother sighed. "You know there is nothing else."

But Ming-li began to take off her *kua tze*. "Here," she said, "wear my jacket. It is newer and is almost large enough."

"No." Su-lan raised her head. "I will go as I am."

"Here, then." Her mother handed an old knitted woolen shawl to her husband. "Cover her with this. She will be very cold riding."

She followed her father out of the room without looking back. Su-lan had often dreamed of going to the city to see the busy lanes of traffic, the stores along the streets, the colorful palace roofs. Now as she left the family, she showed no surprise and said no good-byes. She climbed into the ricksha and covered herself with the old shawl. But as she rode along, she did not feel the pleasure and excitement that she had long looked forward to. She could not enjoy riding while her father ran in front of her between the shafts. The conversation between her father and mother the night before troubled her.

Shivering and disheartened, Su-lan sat huddled under the frayed shawl, but her shifting glance missed little of the strange sights about her. She had no idea where they were going. She knew little of the city except what she had seen from the tower above the wall or what someone had told her.

After a time her father left the winding lanes outside the wall, and they passed under the huge arch of the An Ting Men or Main Gate on the northeast. This must be one of the broad highways that crisscross the city, Su-lan thought. Her father trotted steadily along, threading his way among the people and carriages, ox carts and sedan chairs. Now and then an automobile came honking along shooing everyone out of the way.

But at last she caught a glimpse of the gold tile of the Bell and Drum Towers extending above the gray of the flat one-story buildings. And she remembered the closeness of her brother and sisters under the quilt on the *k'ang* when she had told them the story of the Bell.

Her color-hungry eyes picked out the bright decorations and the garish signs at the entrance of the shops, the embroidery on the banners of the wedding procession, the green of an official sedan chair, the purple harness of a mule pulling a Peking cart, the bright red pillars and green tile roof of the *p'ai lou* under which they passed when they turned into another broad highway. She could not be sad long. All her life she had wanted to see this part of the city. But all too soon her father left the broad highway and entered a *hutung*, narrow and unpaved. But the ricksha glided smoothly and swiftly over the packed dirt lane after her father's steady, tireless running.

High walls, unbroken but for an occasional gateway, lined the *hutung*. The crowds and traffic, the shops and color had been left behind. Su-lan slumped down into the ricksha seat. There was nothing here to see but her father with the old jagged scar across the back of his close-cropped head. The scar, Su-lan remembered, had come from a knife wound he had received in a street fight. His

faded blue cotton jacket, wet with perspiration, billowed out behind him as he ran, showing the cloth that held up his baggy trousers.

Did Father ever tire? Did his feet never get sore? His shoes of heavy black cotton must be worn and old.

It seemed to Su-lan that she had been riding for hours and hours. But at last her father slowed down, and then he stopped beside one of the closed gates. Two empty rickshas stood at one side of the gate, and two coolies squatted beside them, smoking and chatting.

Su-lan's father put down the ricksha shafts, pulled out a piece of dirty rag from his belt, and wiped his face. Turning, he motioned for Su-lan to get out. When he pounded on the gate, an old man with a few sparse white whiskers opened it a crack and peered at the two suspiciously. Apparently satisfied, he opened the gate wide enough for the two to enter.

Su-lan and her father followed the old man into the gatehouse just inside the wall. Here a fire burned in a clay pot. A small table and a straight chair by the window were the only pieces of furniture in the room.

Father turned to Su-lan. "Wait here a moment," he said, and he disappeared with the gateman in the direction of the inner courtyards.

Su-lan held her hands out over the small open fire and then looked around the room. On the wall a picture of a beautiful Chinese girl dressed in a yellow satin gown caught her eye.

She drew in her breath as she looked at the girl in the picture. Such beauty! Someday, she thought—and she let her fancy run free. So absorbed had she become in the Chinese girl that she did not hear the woman and the old gateman come into the room.

"What is your name?" A cold voice brought her back to the present.

Su-lan spun around. The strange woman who had spoken wore a thick fur-lined *i-fu,* or outer garment, more beautiful than anything Su-lan had ever seen before.

"My humble name is Su-lan, honorable Tai Tai [Madam]," the girl answered, not looking up into the face of the woman.

"How old are you?"

"I am eleven years old, Tai Tai."

"Arrangements have been made for you to come with me," the woman said. "You are to be my girl now. Do not ever try to return to your home. You will be severely punished if you do. My name is Fan Tai Tai, and you will come with me to my home."

Su-lan looked up now and saw the woman's face. "What unsmiling eyes!" Su-lan thought. "But she is not bad looking. Her skin is fairer than that of the women of the settlement outside the wall."

The woman motioned, and Su-lan noticed her hands, well cared for, with long, curling, painted nails.

Like claws, the girl thought to herself as she followed Fan Tai Tai out to the gate. She looked around for her father and his ricksha, but only the two remained that had been stationed at the gate when she and her father had arrived.

The woman climbed into one of the rickshas and motioned Su-lan to be seated in the other.

"*Hui chia* [Return home]!" Fan Tai Tai ordered the coolies who sprang between the shafts.

"*Hui chia!*" they shouted to each other as they swung their rickshas around and started to run at an even pace down the lane that Su-lan and her father had come up a short time before.

Su-lan pulled the frayed scarf about her and looked around. There was no sign of her father or his ricksha.

The House on Lantern Street

Lanterns, delicate and fragile as butterflies, some long and slender, some round and bulging, all gay and colorful, hang from long cords above the store entrances and swing lightly in the breeze making Lantern Street in the Chinese City a place of magic and beauty.

The Chinese City lies to the south of the Tartar City which surrounds the Imperial City and the Forbidden City. Like a Chinese box, one city inside another, they make up the great city of Peking. It is in the Chinese City where most of the shops are found.

Many of the gay and busy streets are named after their special shops, such as Embroidery Street, Bronze Street, Silversmiths' Street, Porcelain Street, and many others. On these streets shopkeepers make and sell their product, each trying to outdo the others.

The two coolies, with the rickshas bearing Madam Fan and Su-lan, swung into Lantern Street soon after passing the Ch'ien Men, or Front Gate, in the south wall of the Tartar City. Here they mingled with the noisy, bustling traffic of the narrow lane. Colorful banners and swinging lanterns on each side of the lane seemed almost to touch and make a canopy overhead.

For a moment Su-lan almost forgot to wonder what her fate would be. She had never seen anything so strange and beautful as Lantern Street. But suddenly the ricksha pullers put down their long handles and stepped out of the shafts. Su-lan came to with a start and realized that the ride had ended.

Fan Tai Tai handed several coppers to the coolies, who grumbled and began to argue about the pay. But Madam Fan' turned

27

quickly into the entrance of a lantern shop, pushing Su-lan ahead of her.

"*Lai! Lai!*" She motioned for Su-lan to follow her.

After the sunshine of the street, the room Su-lan entered seemed to her quite dark at first. The only light entering the room came through a small glass display window. As the girl's eyes became accustomed to the lighting, she saw long counters in the room and many lanterns made of silk mounted on carved wood. The lanterns in different shapes and sizes hung from the ceiling. Some lanterns had the shape of birds, while others looked like crabs, jointed beetles, or bumblebees.

Two men dressed in long gowns bowed low to Madam Fan as she ushered Su-lan through the room.

From the front showroom of the store Fan Tai Tai and Su-lan entered the factory room where a number of workers sat at long tables making objects of cheap paper and light bamboo. Light filtered into the room through a bank of paper-covered windows which faced the inner courtyard. Su-lan noticed everything in the room, even the expressionless faces of the workers who seemed to pay no attention as Madame Fan pushed her through the room.

Madam Fan led her through the factory and into the courtyard, then through a narrow stone gateway in the rear wall which opened into another courtyard surrounded by a group of small buildings. They were all alike, much like the low gray buildings in the settlement outside the north wall, Su-lan decided.

Madam Fan pulled the latch in the first door inside the gate. It creaked as it opened shakily on its rusty hinges, admitting them to a warm, close room where an old woman and two men were chatting and laughing as they stood close around a clay pot charcoal stove. But when the door opened, their talk stopped abruptly. They acknowledged Fan Tai Tai's presence with dutiful nods.

"I expected I'd find you in here, you lazy good-for-nothings." Madame Fan looked from one to the other. "Now, Hu, get back to the kitchen right away and help Wang. And you, Chang, bring some tea to my rooms right away."

"Yes, Tai Tai." "Yes, Tai Tai." The two men slipped out the door.

"Amah," Fan Tai Tai addressed the old woman, "this is Su-lan, whom I am allowing to live here for a while. There are many things that she can do—sweep the courtyards, clean out the stoves, empty the water buckets, and scour the kettles for Ma in the kitchen. She will need something better to wear. I want you to go down to Pang's pawnshop and see if you can find a better jacket for her."

Madam Fan turned to go.

"Tai Tai, where is the child to sleep?" the old lady asked.

"Sleep? Oh, you can find a place. Let her sleep with the other slave girls, Pear Blossom and Peony. It doesn't make much difference."

"Tai Tai, do not be angry if I suggest that the older *ya tou* will not like to have her with them. She is unwashed and uncombed. They will put her out."

"This child can take care of herself, I warrant. She can fight for herself. Anyway, Pear Blossom and Peony put on too many airs; this will take them down a trifle." Madam Fan shrugged as she left the room.

Su-lan looked up into Goh Amah's face that was wrinkled like an old apple, her eyes mere slits amid the drooping folds of heavy eyelids. In her white hair drawn severely back from the forehead and made into a knot on top of her head was stuck a metal hook used for cleaning the ears. Then Su-lan noticed the woman's gray cotton jacket and black quilted trousers neatly tied at the ankle with strips of cloth. Her shoes were tiny, not more than five inches long, and her swollen ankles told the story of early foot-binding.

Again Su-lan looked up into the old woman's face and smiled.

"Tough, are you?" the old woman said. "Well, you'll need to be tough to survive in this household. And strong too." She reached for the girl's arms underneath the tattered padded jacket and felt them. "You'll do. You're all wires and muscles. You didn't get that way from sitting on a cushion doing embroidery. But little girls should be soft and plump."

"I don't like to sit and embroider," Su-lan said, sensing at once that this woman would be a friend. "I like to run outdoors, to climb on the wall, to slide on the ice, to play with the children on the moat, to—"

"You lived outside the wall then?"

Su-lan nodded. The old woman looked down at the child's feet, untidy in their wrappings of rags tied around with strips of cotton cloth. Su-lan followed her glance.

"It's been a long time since I had a pair of new shoes," she said. "Mother has so many to make shoes for. And I wear them out so fast," she hurried to add.

"A great girl like you should be able to make your own shoes. I don't suppose that sliding on the ice helps them. But even at that you've been lucky."

"Lucky? What do you mean?" Su-lan asked.

"When I was a little girl, I would have loved to slide on the ice, to run and play. But I spent my time curled up on the, *k'ang* under a quilt, moaning in pain. My feet had to be small enough to win a proper husband, you know." She looked down at the neat slippers and the misshapen ankles. "A stupid idea that a woman my height should have such tiny feet."

"Do they still hurt you?"

"Oh, the pain I had as a child is gone, but gone also is my freedom to move about easily and swiftly. I hobble now like a swaying willow. Our fathers thought the willow walk was beautiful, and they didn't approve of girls going very far out of the home. This was one way of knowing where they were. No climbing walls or running on the ice for us. A pair of shoes would last a long time." Goh Amah sighed, then added slowly, "But—I will teach you to make yourself a pair of shoes."

"Do you think I could?" Su-lan looked up into Goh Amah's eyes. "I hardly know how to hold a needle. And besides, what would I have to make them out of?"

"A few bits of cloth and paper and some paste are all that are necessary. I think we will be able to find these. But now we must do something about that jacket. It will not take me long. I'll get you a hot towel, and you can be cleaning up while I go to the pawnshop."

Goh Amah brought Su-lan a towel on which to wipe her hands and face; then she hurried away to Pang's shop.

The jacket that Goh Amah brought back was not new, but it was clean and warm. Su-lan marveled as she fingered the thicknesses of stout cotton cloth with padding between. But it did not seem suitable to put this good clean garment on over her inner layers of rags. But how could she discard them until she had something to take their place? And besides, her few coppers lay hidden in the cotton, and she had no other place to keep them.

The blue jacket didn't look good with the dirty padded trousers and ragged shoes either, but to Su-lan it did seem a great improvement.

"Now my top half belongs to Fan Tai Tai," she laughed, "and my lower half belongs to the canal."

"Laugh today, little canal girl," the old woman said. "You may be weeping tomorrow."

"I never cry," Su-lan protested. "But is Fan Tai Tai then such a hard mistress?" She had noticed how the workers had acted as the madam passed through the factory, and how Goh Amah and the two men had suddenly stopped their talk when Fan Tai Tai had appeared. But should she, Su-lan, not be grateful to her?

"You will find out." Goh Amah closed her lips as if she had already said too much. "But," she went on after a moment's hesitation, "life will be quite different. Cold and hunger and hard times you may be used to. Yes, even hard work. But you have had freedom, and long hours in which to play. There will be no freedom here and no time to play. It will not be like running on the moat with a flock of little children, with no more guidance than the pigeons that swoop above the city."

A wave of homesickness passed over Su-lan as she thought of the gay free days of the past.

"There, child, I didn't intend to frighten you. You will get along, I'm sure. Anyway, you do not need to think about it until tomorrow. Today you can pretend you are a lady. Right now I want you to sit on this stool by the stove and I will comb your hair. How long and thick it is! You should take better care of it."

Su-lan had never realized the unkempt appearance of her hair. She had never looked in a mirror. There was none in her home, but she sought quickly to make excuses.

"I have no comb, and I was busy with the little children before I left home this morning."

Goh Amah produced a small fine wooden comb from an inside pocket of her jacket. "See, I bought you one. It was only a few coppers. You can pay me back sometime, perhaps."

"Oh, yes, I will." Su-lan's eyes brightened. "Can I have it for my very own?"

"Of course."

When the old woman began to untie the string which fastened the long braid, Su-lan protested. "But no! You must not. I can do it myself."

"This one time, let me do it for you. Sit still and tell me about your games on the moat. And what do you do in summer when there is no ice to slide on?"

Goh Amah began to smooth the tangled and matted braid, combing patiently the long black locks. Meanwhile Su-lan talked about her life in the north city, adventures with her friends, not forgetting the experience of the night before. Was it only last evening that the queer foreigners had come to skate by the old city wall? Su-lan stopped talking and stared into the fire burning in the clay pot.

Now the old woman stopped combing. Su-lan's hair spread out across her shoulders and reached almost to the floor. It shone like burnished ebony.

"Come, little one, tonight you may sleep in my room," Goh Amah broke into Su-lan's thoughts.

The girl got up and followed the old woman. She wondered how Goh Amah had come to be in the Fan household. She seemed something a little more than the ordinary servant. By all the rules she should have been ruling over her own household, Su-lan thought.

As the days went by she learned that Goh Amah had been an obedient daughter, a good wife, a hardworking mother, and then a grandmother. It was, by the custom of the Chinese, her turn to sit back and tell others what to do. To be a servant meant to lose face. But when Goh Amah's husband died, the old lady had had no way to earn a living and had come to the Fan family to care for their infant son, now grown to manhood. Ten years ago the young man had brought his young wife to his father's household. Business had prospered, but no children had been born to them, and then Fan died of the plague. Then the widow took over the business. She had allowed the Amah to remain in the household to do the sewing and mending and to take care of the women servants.

Su-lan learned many things from kindly, gentle Goh Amah.

Su-lan and "The Tiger"

Su-lan followed Goh Amah, listening to the chatter of the servants as they worked. Every day she learned something new about the people around her. One day her eyes grew wide as she heard, *"Hu lai liao!"* She looked around the room. She had heard the expression "tiger's coming" before. It had been used by grown-ups to scare little children into being good.

"But why—?" she started to ask Goh Amah, when everyone stopped talking and began to work furiously. Then she saw Fan Tai Tai standing in the doorway with a grim, determined look. Now Su-lan understood! The servants had nicknamed Fan Tai Tai "The Tiger."

"Whenever she sees us talking together, she seems to think we are talking about her," Goh Amah explained later. "It makes her furious." The old woman chuckled. "The truth is, we usually are talking about her."

"That Pear Blossom and Peony seem to be her most trusted servants," Su-lan said, "but they tell more tales than the others about Fan Tai Tai. I do not trust them. I am glad you did not put me in with those two." Su-lan frowned as she spoke.

But each day Su-lan found the servants friendlier, and she found many things to do to help them. Before long they came to depend on her for many small jobs.

"Bring me a pail of water," Peony called when she wanted to wash a few clothes.

"Su-lan, Su-lan," Wang Shih Fu (cook), shouted, "bring me a pan of charcoal for the stove and then empty these peelings."

Su-lan brought the charcoal and then took the peelings out to

33

the sewer opening outside the back gate of the compound where several dogs scavanged for scraps.

For a moment she would pause to look up and down the dingy alley. It certainly did not look anything like Lantern Street. If only she could visit there again and see the banners and the show windows. But to reach Lantern Street she would have to go through the main courtyard and the shop, and that had been forbidden. Slowly she would turn and go back to the kitchen to fulfill some other command.

Goh Amah comforted her often those first few weeks.

"Are you not tired, child?" she asked Su-lan at the end of the day.

"No, I'm not tired. But I don't like so many people telling me what to do." Then to herself she added, "And I don't intend to be here always."

Because she did her work well, the other servants quickly learned to like and trust her. She began to feel less put upon and noticed that she was not watched so closely.

The compound seemed a maze of courtyards and gateways to Su-lan. Would she ever learn her way around? she asked Goh Amah, who laughed at the problem. "It is enough that you know your way around the kitchen," the Amah replied.

Su-lan often invented errands to take her to the kitchen, the most popular place in the compound for the workers and servants. Smoke from the chimneyless charcoal fires that glowed under huge cauldrons smudged the room. But there was food there—such quantities of food as Su-lan had never seen before.

She could hardly take her eyes off the two long tables upon which Wang Shih Fu and Hu, the Number Two boy, chopped crisp vegetables or arranged platters of food for the family tables. Wang Shih Fu and Hu often gave her bits of food from the table, or they saved leftovers for her. Never in her whole life had Su-lan been so well fed.

There was always warmth in the kitchen, and the continual chatter of small talk from people going and coming. And Wang always noticed Su-lan with a smile, a nod, or a teasing remark. He never asked her to carry heavy loads. Next to Goh Amah, Su-lan liked to be around Wang, the cook.

Outside the kitchen door stood a large earthen jar almost as tall as Su-lan. Each day coolies delivered buckets full of water which they poured into the jar. Su-lan watched to see when Wang or Hu needed more water for cooking or washing dishes. Then she would hurry to the big earthen jar and dip out the water for them.

One day while Wang Shih Fu and Hu enjoyed a little idle talk, and Hu, who could never talk and work at the same time, laid down his knife with which he had been cutting bamboo sprouts into thin slices, Su-lan picked up the knife and quietly continued the slicing, making quick, short movements away from her as Hu had been doing.

"See, the little *ya tou* is clever with her fingers," Hu remarked.

At the words *ya tou,* Su-lan's anger flared. She threw down the knife. "I am not a slave girl. My name is Su-lan." She tossed her head, swinging her long braid in a wide arc. Then she dashed from the room like an enraged animal.

Wham! She ran headlong into Fan Tai Tai coming into the kitchen at that moment.

Su-lan drew back, horrified. *"Ai-yah, ai-yah,"* she stammered. "I'm sorry. I didn't mean to—" she started to apologize.

"Take care where you're going, you little gutter rat, you—" Madam Fan interrupted, and, reaching out, she slapped Su-lan on the cheek. Her fingers with their long curving nails carved a deep scratch on Su-lan's cheek. The girl staggered from the blow. Slowly she straightened up and put her hand up to her face and felt a sticky dampness. Then looking at her hand she saw it streaked with blood. Never before had anyone laid a hand on her in anger.

She had often quarreled with the other children in their rough play beside the moat. But they had never hit each other in real anger. But now, a flood of words, the language of the canal people, poured into her mind and almost escaped her lips. But for some unaccountable reason she stood silent.

"Someday things will be different," she vowed to herself. "This is not the time—but—"

"Chu-ba!" Fan Tai Tai motioned with her hand. "Go to your room, and no supper for you tonight."

Then she shouted at Wang Shih Fu and Hu. "Get to your work! Don't stand here as if a juggler were performing. There is much to do. We are having three guests this evening."

Su-lan went to her room as Fan Tai Tai had commanded. Later, when Goh Amah came to the room, Su-lan told her the story. The old lady sponged the swollen cheek and told of the time that Pear Blossom had come into conflict with her mistress.

"Pear Blossom," Goh Amah said, "took a pair of jade earrings from Fan Tai Tai's room. She planned to wear them when she went home for a visit and then return them, or so she said. But when Madam missed them, Pear Blossom denied knowledge of their whereabouts, hoping to get them back into the jewel case. However, Madam made a search and found the earrings in the lining of the sleeve of Pear Blossom's best jacket.

"Fan Tai Tai beat her with her round bamboo cane and locked her in the punishment room for three days," Goh Amah continued.

"How did she get out?" Su-lan asked.

"Oh, after three days Madam Fan needed her so badly that she told her she would let her out and would not report to the police, if Pear Blossom would *kowtow* to her and apologize."

"And did she?"

"Oh, yes, of course." Goh Amah nodded.

"She did wrong to take the earrings," Su-lan said. "But I would never kowtow to Madam Fan, no matter what."

"No, I don't believe you would. But in that case, you will have to watch where you are going before you go rushing into people because you are so angry."

"I guess I shouldn't get angry so quickly," Su-lan said. "And I shouldn't have minded because Hu called me a *ya tou*. But he could have used some other word. Some *ya tous*, you know—"

Goh Amah nodded.

"Anyway," Su-lan went on, "I don't intend to be a *ya tou* very long."

"Brave words, indeed. And what do you think you can do about it?"

"I won't stay here!" Su-lan stomped her foot.

"Child, child, do not think or dream of running away. It is impossible. 'He who has no diamond should not attempt to cut glass.' Even if you should manage to get away from here, what would you do? Would you go back to your father's home?"

"Oh, never! That's the first place Madam Fan would look for

me. And besides—" She hesitated. "And besides, *he* might bring me back again," she said in a low voice. "No, I will never go home. I made up my mind to that when I left."

"You wouldn't beg, would you? Beggars flourish in Peking and make a comfortable living. There is a large beggars' guild, and the members are protected and—"

Su-lan looked up at Goh Amah in surprise. "You are not serious, are you, Goh Amah?" But seeing the serious look on the old woman's face, Su-lan flushed. "Just because I may have looked like a beggar when I came here, you don't need to think—" and she commenced a rapid denunciation of the amah and of begging.

Then Su-lan saw a slow smile come into the old woman's eyes. She stopped. "You fooled me that time."

But the old woman did not seem ready to drop the subject yet. "Let me warn you," she waggled her bony finger at Su-lan. "Don't try anything foolish. You may have some hidden charm that I know not of, but for the life of me I cannot imagine what a little girl of your age would do on her own in a big city like Peking. If you stayed on the streets, the police would pick you up in no time and would probably bring you back here. You might find some place to hide, but you couldn't stay hidden forever. You would have to eat. You would have to sleep. After all, it isn't so bad here. At least you won't starve or freeze, and you have a place to sleep."

"Yes, that's so," Su-lan acknowledged. "And I have you, and that is the best of all. But I don't intend to spend the rest of my life here, and you can count on that. Just how soon I shall have to think up a plan I don't know. Maybe you can help me think of something."

Goh Amah shook her head. "Don't ask me to help you. The very idea frightens me."

Dumplings and Lanterns

Before the red line on Su-lan's cheek had faded to pink and finally disappeared, the most important time of the year had come —the New Year celebration. Everyone in Madam Fan's establishment, whether in the showroom, factory, or kitchen, had been extra busy for days. Su-lan found many chores to do. Everyone called on her to help.

Now the kitchen became the center of ceaseless activity, where dishes of all varieties were prepared in advance and reserved for the holiday feasts. Even Peony and Pear Blossom helped when it came to the big job, on the last day of the year, of wrapping the *pao-tze* or boiled dumplings which would be eaten at midnight, when there would be fireworks and much laughter.

A feeling of festivity and excitement had spread from the streets and shops and front reception rooms to the workers and servants in kitchens and rear courtyards.

Fan Tai Tai's lantern business flourished. Two weeks after New Year's Day came the Feast of Lanterns. No one wanted to be without lanterns for this holiday celebration. Business in the shop kept Fan Tai Tai too busy to check on the kitchen as she usually did. The servants, knowing that "The Tiger" would not be likely to come into the kitchen, laughed and chatted as they worked.

On the work tables the servants chopped and minced meats and vegetables for the filling for the dumplings. It had to be fine and smooth enough to satisfy the particular Wang Shih Fu. He did the kneading and rolling of the dough himself, for if it were too stiff, it would not shape properly, and if too soft, it would not hold the filling when dropped into the boiling water.

Peony and Pear Blossom giggled a good deal while trying to wrap the dumplings. The dough stuck to their fingers, and the girls spent much time scraping it off. Again and again they rolled the dough, each time making it stiffer and stiffer. Wang showed them again and again how to fill each small circle of dough, fold it over, and pinch the edges.

"Now let me try it again," Peony laughed, showing her dimples. "I don't see how you can make them without their sticking to your fingers."

Wang smiled at her as if he didn't mind how much she got mixed up with the dumplings. "You have a dab of flour on the end of your nose, and a piece of dough stuck to your elbow," he laughed. *"K'an shih jung i, tso shih nan* [Looking is easy, but doing is hard]," he said, quoting the proverb. "Now watch me. I will show you once more." He took one of the thin flat circles of dough on the palm of his hand.

"Now place a small lump of the filling just slightly off-center —so," he continued, while deftly lifting the right amount with a pair of chopsticks. "Now fold the dough over and pinch the edges together, giving the dumpling a slight jog with each pinch, so that when you finish it has the shape of a small pouch with a crinkled lid."

Su-lan watched. Peony couldn't seem to get the hang of it. Her little plate of dumplings held a queer assortment of different shapes, some flat, some oozing forth their insides where the edges came apart. Pear Blossom's were only slightly better. Su-lan worked on hers again, her small slim fingers moved swiftly, pinching and turning the dough.

"Look at Su-lan's! We can serve *hers* to the guests. They are perfect," Wang Shih Fu said.

"Of course, we are not accustomed to kitchen work," Pear Blossom pouted.

"Cheer up! There'll be more for us to eat," Hu announced.

Everyone laughed. Even though they did not always share in the delicacies made for the family and guests, everyone knew that at this season there would be plenty for all.

Su-lan watched Wang put the dumplings into the boiling water. She thought of one New Year when her mother had bought some dumplings from the outdoor food store. They had been coarse, and the pastry tough and gluey. But these! Su-lan's mouth watered as Wang lifted the tiny delicate dumplings from the kettle.

While the making of the *pao-tze* went on, Pear Blossom and Peony brought gossip and news of the outside world. They reported interesting events in the showroom or the workshop, or repeated conversations they had heard between Madam Fan and her nephews, or with *K'ung*, the foreman of the shop.

"One of those queer foreigners came in to buy a lamp yesterday." Pear Blossom giggled.

Su-lan stopped folding the *pao-tze* dough and looked up at Pear Blossom.

"What a sight!" Pear Blossom went on. "His face had a reddish, weatherbeaten look. He had bushy eyebrows with flecks of white in them." She giggled again. "But his whiskers! Short and bushy on his upper lip, and more on his chin. Not long white ones like our venerables wear, but crisp and clipped and scrubby."

"How old a man was he?" Hu asked.

"What did he want?" Wang Shih Fu wanted to know.

Su-lan said nothing, but she listened the more intently.

"Oh, I probably couldn't guess his age within a hundred years," Pear Blossom answered. "You know, you can never guess the age of foreigners.

"This man rode up in a fine private ricksha with brass lanterns and his own coolie. He wore a fine heavy overcoat like his people all wear. Lan Li expected he might sell him one of his best silk lamps with a carved teakwood frame. Of course Lan Li began to wonder how much he could ask and get from such an obviously rich man.

"Lan greeted him in his very best English, and asked him what he could show him, but this fellow sort of grunted and started looking around at this lamp and that, feeling the silk and studying the patterns. Lan politely tried to find out what he wanted, and just about exhausted all the English he knew, when the man turned and began to speak Chinese rapidly, describing the kind of lamp he wanted.

"You should have seen the look on Lan's face. After he had displayed all the English he knew, this foreigner talked in Chinese!"

"But you didn't tell us what the man was really looking for," several of the servants protested.

"Oh, well, he wanted a shade to go on some foreign lampstand. He wanted one shaped like one in the shop but made with the same material as another, and the pattern of still another." Pear Blossom paused. "The amazing thing was the way he spoke Chinese," she went on. "If you hadn't seen his face, you would have thought it was one of our own people talking."

"Is that all?" Wang Shih Fu scoffed. "I thought the man wanted to buy the shop itself."

"Did he get his shade?" Su-lan spoke up.

"No, not then. Of course they didn't have one in the shop like he wanted. Lan told him they would make one up according to his directions, but he would have to wait until after the Feast of Lanterns, as the shop would be closed most of the time between now and then. The man insisted that he would have to have it sooner than that. He said he'd pay extra if they would do the job at once. Then he pulled out his purse and handed Lan a bill, and said he'd pay more when he came in for the lamp. Lan said the man had a beautiful watch on a chain and that his purse bulged with money."

"Oh, these foreigners are just loaded with money." He shrugged his shoulders.

"Yes, I know," piped up Su-lan. She thought of the man she had seen on the moat and how he had tossed money away.

The group around the tables broke into loud laughter. "Oh, yes, she knows! Ha! Ha!" they whooped. "Sure, she knows."

Su-lan flushed, but she kept still.

"Actually, though," Wang Shih Fu spoke up, "these foreigners are not so uncommon. There are a great many in Peking now. I have a friend who works for one in the American Legation. He told me a lot of tall tales, I'm sure, about their peculiar ways and about some of the things they have. He said they have a big white box in the kitchen that makes ice! They don't have to buy ice, but can take it out of this big white box in little cubes already cut."

"And what would they do with the little cubes already cut? Surely they don't eat them!" Peony giggled.

"No, stupid one. They put them in their drinks. They drink more cold things than hot, you know."

"But the amazing thing about this machine," he continued, "is that it takes heat to make this ice. The machine is run by the same *tien* that is used for lights and telephones, and so on."

"Now, we really don't believe you," one of the girls said. Everyone laughed at the idea of a machine run by electricity to make ice cubes. "Of all notions, heat making ice! It just doesn't make sense."

New Year's Day at Madam Fan's came and went. Su-lan thought she would never forget the gaiety and the festivities of that day. Two weeks later came the Feast of Lanterns.

It had been some time before this that Su-lan had found out how to get to Lantern Street from the rear entrance of Madam Fan's establishment, and on rare occasions she had slipped out to enjoy the interesting sights of the shop windows, and the passing throngs.

Peony and Pear Blossom had gradually left off their haughty attitude toward her, and since the cook had started to call Su-lan *"Mei Mei* (Little Sister)" after having called her the *ya-tou,* the girls began to call her "Mei Mei" also. Su-lan began to have more of a feeling of security.

"Come with us tonight, Mei Mei," Peony invited on the fifteenth day of the new year. "Everyone, absolutely everyone, will be out with lanterns tonight. The streets will be full of people. There will be stilt walkers and processions and street shows of all kinds."

Su-lan, her eyes shining, looked up at Peony. "Thank you! Thank you!" Then, rubbing the sleeve of her jacket with her thumb, she hesitated. "But—but I don't have anything nice to wear. It would not be suitable for me to go along with you."

"You are quite a mess," Pear Blossom agreed. Then, turning to Peony, she said, "Don't you have anything she can wear? Come to think of it, you're about the same size, if not the same shape."

"My gray gown with the fuschia braid might do," Peony offered. "It's almost worn out, anyway. We won't be leaving until after Fan Tai Tai and her guests have gone out this evening. Come to our room then, and we'll see how it goes, Mei Mei."

Su-lan rushed through her chores that afternoon and evening, even skipping over a few. Then she hurried to the room Pear Blosson and Peony shared. In the doorway Su-lan stopped and stared at the two girls. They had smoothed a white paint over their faces.

Touches of red glowed on their cheeks and lips. Pear Blossom pinned a paper flower in Peony's hair.

"How's that?" Pear Blossom asked.

"Oh, how nice," Su-lan exclaimed from the doorway.

"Come in! Come in!" Peony called. "Here's the gray dress. Let's see how it fits."

The girls helped Su-lan into the dress and buttoned it up the sides.

"It's a trifle long, but it will do," Peony nodded. "Now, what about a little makeup for Mei Mei?"

While the girls made up her face, putting a dab of white paint on her forehead and smoothing it out, Su-lan watched in the mirror. Pear Blossom put a touch of red on her cheekbones. Peony combed and oiled her hair until it lay as smooth as black satin.

Su-lan smiled at herself in the mirror. She turned her head this way and that to see the sides trimmed with pieces of yellow yarn.

The older girls laughed at Su-lan and teased her, telling her she would be henceforth useless for carrying water and emptying pails.

Ready at last, the three girls went out the rear gate of Madam Fan's place and wandered into the magic of the moonlit night in Lantern Street. They mingled with the merrymakers and the moving crowds. Rickshas and carriages hurried past. The avenue sparkled with lights, stretching on and on, as far as one could see. Large square lanterns hung over the street from poles, some twelve feet high. Oblong lanterns hung below on either side. Scenes from ancient legends, historical or imaginary, painted on the sides of the thin paper panels showed up clearly against the light from inside.

The shopkeepers on the street had each tried to outdo the others in decorating their shops with their displays of lanterns of all shapes and sizes and colors.

Many of the pedestrians carried weird-shaped lanterns on the end of poles. These moving lighted lanterns made it appear that birds and fish were passing and repassing in all directions.

"Oh, look at that one," Su-lan shouted above the noise of the crowd. "It's a big orange fish with fire spitting from its mouth."

The girls, laughing and talking and looking at everything, sauntered down the street. Once they were swept into a crowd of people and could go neither backward nor forward. Then as the crowd began to thin, they saw a procession of stilt walkers coming along the avenue. Later a dragon, a huge affair carried by a number of concealed carriers, crawled along, belching smoke from its gaping jaws.

Altogether it was a never-to-be-forgotten evening. This was the one evening in the year when women were allowed to walk freely on the streets and mix with the crowds.

The girls stopped at a candy vendor's cart.

Peony and Pear Blossom bought three tart glazed apples on sticks. Su-lan, thinking of her long-treasured coppers, decided to buy some thin rice cookies to share with her friends. She pulled out her coppers.

"Well, Mei Mei!" Peony said in astonishment. "Where on earth did you get the wealth?"

"Not from Fan Tai Tai!" Su-lan answered quickly. Then, seeing their surprise and questioning eyes, she gave one of her loud hearty laughs.

"Not so loud, child," Pear Blossom cautioned. "You'll have everyone looking at us."

Tussle With "The Tiger"

After the holiday season everyone in Fan Tai Tai's household seemed cross and out of sorts. The glimpse into fairyland being over, it was hard to settle down to everyday routine. But gradually the feeling of disenchantment wore off as the Lantern Street shop returned to normal.

Su-lan, having returned the gray gown with the fuchsia braid and the paper flowers, found her work hard now, the pots and pans heavy, and the smelly garbage more distasteful than ever. She tried to perform her tasks as usual, but she became more aloof and spoke in an abrupt manner or in a sharp tone of voice as if she no longer cared to please anyone.

And then came the time of the opening of the buds and the warm days of spring. The thought of green trees and mild breezes brought back memories of her old freedom and the happy times at the moat. Soon the willows would unfold their graceful sprays of green over the water, and the pleasure boats would glide along on the canal. Then the lotus would appear in strong curled shoots. She thought of her brother and sisters at home and how they clamored for her stories that she had heard from the storytellers on the pleasure boats. She thought of her mother sitting on the k'ang by the small charcoal fire. Then she tried to put the thoughts out of her head. She would never go back. She would never think of home.

Peking in spring burst forth as from a giant cocoon. Pushing out of its dry and outworn shell, it emerged like a butterfly of brilliant colors. But on many of the spring days driving winds swept down from the Gobi Desert, bringing clouds of yellow dust to drop on the city. Layers of grit and dirt lay thick over everything, penetrating

45

all the cracks of the houses, respecting no one, rich or poor. Then no one dared to go out on the streets without a heavy veil over his face; and indoors, people kept busy with brooms and dusters.

On such a day Su-lan, on crossing the courtyard from the kitchen to Goh Amah's room, met Pear Blossom with a worried frown on her face.

"Oh, Su-lan, you're just the one I'm looking for. I need you. Are you busy right now? I'd like you to help me if you will." Pear Blossom caught at Su-lan's sleeve.

"Why, what's the matter, has anything happened?" Su-lan asked.

"Well, you know Peony is sick, and I've had her work to do as well as my own, and I've had things to do for her besides. I've been busy all day, and I should make her some thin rice gruel, but this storm came up, and everything's covered with dust in Madam Fan's apartment. It will take hours for me to clean it up alone, and I thought may—"

Su-lan had never been inside Fan Tai Tai's apartment. "Would you like me to help you?" she asked quickly. "Would Madam Fan care?"

Pear Blossom shrugged. "She's out right now and will never know. Come on and be a good Mei Mei."

They hurried over the paving stones and entered the door to Madam Fan's rooms.

"Just look." Pear Blossom closed the door behind them and stood with her arms outstretched.

Su-lan stared, not at the film of dust on the tables, chairs, and floor, but at the stately elegance of the series of rooms, like a string of beads. Each room opened up from the vestibule. Open latticework of carved wood edged the doorways between the rooms; silk panels and graceful paintings of birds and flowers hung from the walls; bamboo mattings covered the floors except for the *k'o t'ing* (reception room). There a thick wool carpet in soft shades of buff and blue with swirling sprays of flowers and symbols around the border covered the floor.

"Oh, it's beautiful!" Su-lan exclaimed.

"Yes, but it means a lot of work," Pear Blossom complained. She handed Su-lan a soft cloth.

"Be careful not to break anything. Every single vase will have to be lifted and dusted, and every one of the *pai-shê* [bric-a-brac] wiped off and dusted underneath."

Su-lan's eyes took in everything in the room. Here were some of the madam's finest pieces of art. She picked up a cloisonné vase and turned it to see the delicate colors. As she dusted each piece, she noticed the details of workmanship, the intricate carving of a lacquer tray, the sheen of a porcelain jar. Carefully wiping and polishing, she returned each piece to its position on table or stand.

Little glass cases held some of the finer pieces of art. She touched the glass with her fingertips and then rubbed it vigorously so that not a fingerprint nor a speck of dust would remain. How could Pear Blossom be so callous to all this beauty? These things seemed to mean nothing to her; she hurried so at her work. But Su-lan walked slowly across the room to the small altar with the ancestral tablets on it and a small incense burner and candlesticks.

Now she thought of the day when she had stopped at the door of a small Taoist temple outside the wall and peered inside at the crumbling dust-draped figures hardly visible in the dark. But she had stepped out quickly when a priest appeared in the background and started to walk toward her. She could remember now the depressing sight and odor of musty garments and stale incense.

Su-lan paused briefly to observe Fan Tai Tai's altar to her ancestors, but Pear Blossom sharply reminded her to get on with her job.

The girl sighed as she went about her work. Finally she came to the last of the series of rooms, the sleeping apartment of Fan Tai Tai. Long drapes, now drawn back with cords, curtained the platform bed built in a recessed alcove. The quilted coverlets in bright colors lay neatly folded at one side of the bed.

"Come, come, Mei Mei," Pear Blossom urged Su-lan. "I must get back to Peony." Then, looking around, she added, "There's not much more to do now. You won't mind working alone for a few minutes, will you? I'll run back to the room for just a minute. I want to start cooking the gruel for Peony."

Su-lan hardly noticed when Pear Blossom spoke. She stood entranced before the boudoir cabinet and all the small intriguing articles on it.

" 'He who has seen little, marvels much,' " Pear Blossom said as she hurried out of the room.

One by one Su-lan moved the little bottles and jars and tiny metal boxes as she dusted the cabinet.

What could all these covered containers have inside? Cosmetics for the madam's toilet, no doubt. She marveled at the number and variety of them. If only she dared to peek inside some of the containers! A small china bowl with painted chrysanthemums and peonies on the side caught her fancy. She held the fragile bowl in her hands and then carefully lifted the lid.

Could it be empty? She pressed her fingers down into the bowl. Three keys lay on the bottom. Only three keys! Su-lan placed the bowl back in the cabinet.

She reached for a slender-throated vial no larger than a bird's egg and lifted the stopper. The fragrance of a thousand flowers rushed into the room. She lifted the stopper to her nose and breathed in the fragrance; then, carefully replacing the stopper, she put the vial back in its place. A small white jar contained a strange green ointment. Su-lan touched the ointment with her fingertips. Then she rubbed a little between her fingers. It felt smooth and smelled sweet. She took another dab and spread it on her hands.

Beside the cabinet, on an elegant dressing table of carved teakwood, stood a small mirror framed in brass.

"Oh, how beautiful!" Su-lan exclaimed, and slowly as if in a dream she sat down on the stool before the dressing table and looked at her reflection in the glass.

She looked a long time. This face in the mirror did not please her. It was broad, not oval and pointed; the cheekbones high; the lips too full; the almond-shaped eyes too far apart under thick eyebrows. Her hair, which had looked so smooth the night of the Feast of Lanterns, now looked scraggly and dull, although she had carefully braided it that morning.

Su-lan pulled the wooden comb Goh Amah had bought for her out of her jacket, and smoothed the loose ends. Could the green ointment in the white jar be hair pomade? She experimented smoothing a trifle on her hair over the temple and brows, and combed again and again until her hair looked shiny black.

"That's much better," she said out loud, turning her head this way and that. "Now, let me see—" She picked up the small hand mirror on the table and examined her skin at close range. "Ugh," she exclaimed. "There are marks on my cheeks from the sickness I had many years ago." She remembered how completely they had been hidden when Peony and Pear Blossom had painted her cheeks for the Lantern Festival. What kind of stuff had they put on? Maybe she would find some here among Madam Fan's toilet articles.

She peeked into a few more of the small containers and found a cake of white powder. Ah, ha! This must be it, she thought, and applied a little with her fingers, quickly spreading it on her cheeks. The effect so startled her that she threw back her head and burst into a loud laugh. The laugh rang through the empty rooms and made her jump, reminding her where she was and what she was doing. Pear Blossom might be back any minute. She glanced in the mirror once more. Her laughter froze, for coming through the door behind her she saw Fan Tai Tai, the "tiger" look on her face as she swept through the apartment.

Su-lan sprang up from the stool and grabbed her dustcloth, although she realized the futility of pretending to be at work.

"What do you mean, you little vagabond, sitting here in my bedroom, at my table, handling my things, you—" Fan Tai Tai's words lashed out at Su-lan in cold fury.

"Pear Blossom needed some help after the dust storm, and I haven't hurt a thing, really, I just—"

But Fan Tai Tai screamed, "Just like the little turtle's egg that you are to come crawling in here when I am out, and make yourself at home like a grand lady."

Su-lan knew she had no right to touch any of the toilet articles other than to dust them. She knew she had no right to sit at the mistress's table. At first she felt repentant and remorseful. But as Fan Tai Tai continued to scream at her and the words of abuse piled up and those long slim fingers flew at Su-lan's face, she put up her arms to defend herself. Then her complete vocabulary of bad language, the language of the canal, came flooding into her mind. To apologize would be useless, and explanations would be of no avail. The girl had no defense but her tongue, so she answered back name for name.

Fan Tai Tai drew from a hidden spot in the cabinet a short bamboo rod and began to strike Su-lan on the head. Blow after blow fell on the victim until the blood ran down her hot red face.

Then, clutching the girl by the thick braid, Madam Fan pushed and dragged her back through the rooms, out the door, and across the courtyard.

Out of the corner of her eye, Su-lan saw Pear Blossom enter the courtyard. Surely she would speak up in Su-lan's defense! But Su-lan saw the look of fright on Pear Blossom's face, and in a moment the girl slunk out of sight behind the gate.

Madam Fan pushed Su-lan into a small cubicle, originally a storeroom for brooms and garden equipment. The clicking sound after the door had been shut told Su-lan that she had been locked in this room that had been used more than once as a prison for slaves or servants who had brought upon themselves the anger of the madam.

But surely Pear Blossom would tell Madam Fan that she had asked Su-lan to help her. Su-lan huddled in the corner. What she had done, she knew Pear Blossom could not undo for her.

Pear Blossom, hiding behind the gate, peeked around at the sound of the door slamming.

"How did *she* get back so soon? I am sure she said she would be gone all evening," she mused. Then she began to guess at what had happened when she left Su-lan in the madam's room. But she didn't intend to get herself mixed up with this in any way.

Pear Blossom waited until Madam Fan, having locked the door of the cubicle, returned to her apartment; then she hurriedly slipped back to her room. She would pretend she knew nothing of the affair.

Pear Blossom didn't mention the episode to anyone but Peony, whom she swore to secrecy. Yet somehow, by evening everyone in the servants' quarters seemed to know what had happened to Su-lan, although no one seemed to know just why she was there.

"Probably told the old lady off," Ho suggested. "She surely could do it."

"I'd like to have seen and heard it myself," Wang said, puffing on his long pipe.

"The child has too sharp a tongue at times," Goh Amah commented. "I've been afraid it would get her into trouble. 'A pointed tongue, though sharp, makes an insufficient shield,'" she quoted the old proverb. "I wonder what really happened."

That evening when the courtyards were deserted, the old woman crept noiselessly across the stone pavement, through the gate into the next enclosure, and tapped softly at the wooden door of the prison room.

"Su-lan! Su-lan!" she whispered.

"Yes?" a low voice came from the dark cubicle.

"Are you all right, Mei Mei? Are you hurt?"

"Not much. Just my head. It is sore." She did not tell of the terrible pain which had followed the blows of the bamboo cane, and the difficulty she had had to stop the bleeding.

"Tell me what happened," the amah spoke softly.

Su-lan told the whole story, even the part that had so provoked Madam Fan.

"I was very bad, wasn't I?" she asked when she concluded.

"I'm surprised that you would talk that way to an older woman. How could you? That was thoughtless and unwise. And then Fan Tai Tai did not know that Pear Blossom had asked you to go there to help with the dusting, and—"

"But I told her," Su-lan broke in.

"Yes, you told her. You told her much too much. You should have been silent and let her have her say. Then you would have nothing to be sorry for."

"But I'm not sorry," Su-lan insisted stubbornly. "She had no right to call me a turtle's egg or to strike me. I had done nothing wrong. Well, not so very bad, anyway."

"It is never right to return insults no matter what has been said. A real lady knows how to be calm and quiet at all times."

"You are terribly disappointed in me, aren't you?" Su-lan asked.

"No, Mei Mei." The amah seemed to measure her words. "But sad that this has happened. Your life here will be impossible now. Fan Tai Tai will never forget."

"Neither will I. And I'll never tell her I'm sorry. Never! She can keep me in here ten thousand years, and I'll never tell her." Su-lan stomped her foot.

"Ai-yah! Ai-yah! do not say that," the old woman moaned. "Do not be so sure. It is not pleasant being shut in a tiny dark room. But I must go now. Someone might hear us."

"Will you come back tomorrow night?" Su-lan asked in a small voice that had lost its defiance.

"Tomorrow night, if I can," Goh Amah promised. She hurried away, almost bumping into Wang Shih Fu in the inner courtyard.

When the amah told Wang her fears about Su-lan, he shook his head. "Oh, she'll give in eventually and kowtow," he predicted. "Why, she'll have to. What else can she do? You know Fan Tai Tai will not give in. And the child can't stay cooped up in there all the rest of her life."

"But you don't know how determined she is. She says she'll never kowtow. And I think she means it. I'm afraid she'll get sick staying in that dark room, crying and—" Goh Amah's voice trembled as she spoke.

"Crying? Rubbish. Did you ever see Su-lan cry? That girl isn't the crying kind. I don't think she has a tear in her. Now you just rest your heart."

"But she must be cold and hungry—"

"She's used to it. Does no one feed the girl?" Wang began to get excited himself. "Not even 'The Tiger' would dare starve her, would she?"

"She probably takes her something. I don't know. She has the key, and no one else goes in. I must ask Su-lan." The amah shuffled away to her room.

Every day when the servants could talk for a few minutes they talked about Su-lan and wondered how long she could hold out. They knew too that Fan Tai Tai herself seemed more piqued as the days went by, and it appeared that Su-lan would remain indefinitely in prison. The servants shook their heads. This was not the usual result obtained from Madam Fan's system of punishment. Having once stated the conditions of release, she could not change them without losing face. Would Su-lan be given more strokes with the bamboo cane to make her relent?

As the days passed one by one, Su-lan became more and more determined not to give in. Now she kept up her courage by making plans to escape.

Her head healed, but the clotted blood had dried in her matted hair. If only she could comb it out. If only she had some of Madam Fan's hair pomade that she kept on her dressing table, the table with all the jars!

And suddenly Su-lan thought of something that made her smile even in her dark prison room. Perhaps she could get Goh Amah to help her! All the rest of the day she looked forward to the old woman's coming to see her.

"How long is this going to last?" moaned the old woman when she came on the fourth night.

"That is up to you," Su-lan answered calmly.

"What do you mean?" Goh Amah gasped.

"That's what I mean. You must find a way to let me out. I'll never kowtow to Fan Tai Tai! You don't want me to spend the rest of my life in here, do you?"

"No, but it's impossible for me to let you out. What can I do?"

"Why is it impossible? What kind of lock is there on this door?"

"It is bolted and padlocked. The door is very strong. I'm sure you could not break it no matter how hard you tried."

"I know. I've tried that. But listen to me. I have an idea."

"Oh, child, do not think of such frightening ideas." The old lady heaved a sigh. "I am sure there is no way for you to escape. You must give in to the woman."

"No! No! You can help me. I just remembered something today. In the small flowered jar on the cabinet beside Fan Tai Tai's dressing table are some keys. It is quite probable that the one to this lock is among them. Tell Pear Blossom, and ask her to get it. You don't need to do a thing yourself. Get Wang Shih Fu to unlock the door at midnight tomorrow, and let me out the back gate. Fan Tai Tai wouldn't dare beat Wang. She won't even know who did it if you're all careful. Do you think Wang Shih Fu would do that for me?"

Goh Amah hesitated. "Perhaps he would be willing. But what if you should get out the gate? What will you do then? Fan Tai Tai will have the police looking for you everywhere. It will be worse than ever for you if they bring you back."

"I've thought of all that. I've had plenty of time to think. If I once get out the gate, I'll manage. Please help me, Goh Amah!"

"Is there anything you would like to take with you if this improbable plan should work out?"

"Yes, my old shawl that I brought when I came."

Su-lan knew that the House of Lanterns was not far from the moat on the south side of the city, and near the moat were *usually* piles of refuse, caved-in lean-tos, and crumbling shacks left by refugees from flood and war. There she might find a hole to crawl into and hide. The shawl would come in handy. If she could only get out the gate, she would be equal to anything.

She listened as Goh Amah hobbled away. Would she ever see her again? But she could not think of that now. If Wang Shih Fu unlocked her prison door, she would be free!

Out Into the Night

The long hours of the next day passed slowly. Would Wang Shih Fu bring the key? Su-lan pressed her face against the wall of her prison and waited. Night fell. Still Su-lan waited. The mournful howl of a dog, probably out by the open sewer, made her sigh. Shortly after midnight she heard the sound of footsteps shuffling across the courtyard. She stood up, her heart beating fast. Without a word she listened to someone fumbling with the lock on the door. Slowly the door opened, and Su-lan slipped out. She felt her shawl placed over her shoulders. Her rescuer did not speak, but Su-lan heard the sound of the bolt being fastened again. She watched the shadowy figure disappear across the courtyard. Then the child stood alone in the dark narrow *hutung* behind the compound. A shiver passed over her, and she held her shawl close to her and looked up at the stars.

How good the fresh air smelled! It smelled of spring and opening leaves. She looked up at the sky. The moon had been almost full on the New Year when she and Pear Blossom and Peony had walked through the streets. She wished there were a moon now, but of course the tiny curl of a new moon had already set. It would be some time before life would stir in the city, before light would come into the sky and the shopkeepers would push back the shutters from their shop windows. It would be hours before Fan Tai Tai would discover the empty cubicle and alert the police. Why, sometimes the madam slept until noon. That would give Su-lan additional hours of daylight.

Being alone in the streets at night did not bother her. Prowlers were rare; murders were unheard of in the capital city of China at that time. High walls and locked gates helped to keep burglars out of the compounds. Darkness gave the child no concern; rather she needed to find a place to hide. More than once she thought of trying to find work in the home of one of the foreigners who lived in the city. Many of them used Chinese help, she knew. Perhaps she could look after their children. Then she looked down at her soiled and now ragged jacket. Who would hire her like this? Besides, what could she do without any recommendations? But the thought that the police would soon be on her trail made her realize that she must think fast and act quickly.

First of all she knew she had to put as much distance as possible between her and Madam Fan's place. She would hurry to Lantern Street and go east. By that route she would come to the main thoroughfare which led out through the Ch'ien Men, the front gate of the Tartar City. She had come this way by ricksha when Madam Fan had brought her to the Lantern Shop several months ago. How far would it be on foot? Would she reach the gate before daylight?

It would be much farther and more roundabout, of course, than if she went directly north through the back alleys and lanes which filled the space between the wall and Lantern Street like a maze. But she knew better than to get lost in that labyrinth in the darkness. Why, she might follow indefinitely down one dead-end lane after another, and entirely lose her sense of direction. She had heard stories about children losing their way.

Su-lan looked all around her. Then she started out at a trot, at last arriving at Lantern Street. By now she had slowed to a walking pace. The street looked so different from the way it had been two weeks ago, she noted. Then there had been a full moon and the added light from a myriad of lamps. Gone were the lights and the crowds and the noise and the traffic. The lanterns that had dangled in front of the shops had been removed, and the fronts of the display windows were boarded up. At widely spaced intervals street lamps gave a dim circle of light, but the street was deserted. Not even a dog wandered down the road, only the solitary child. And she would be spotted immediately by anyone that might venture onto the street. If only it were daylight. Then she could mingle with the crowds. Her heart beat faster. Anyone, just anyone at all

might see her and wonder what she was doing there. Su-lan began
to run.

Although hungry and weak from lack of food, she seemed to
gain strength from desperation and determination to get away from
Lantern Street and with it the grim Madam Fan.

Stillness hung all around like an empty house. She could run no
farther. Su-lan slowed her steps, but the beating of her heart and
her muffled footsteps even in her soft shoes made her look back
several times to see if pursuers were after her. Once she heard
voices from behind the wall—the high-pitched tones of a man and
a woman arguing. The words she could not hear, but she began
to run again, and the sound faded out as she continued down the
street.

Just when she became aware of the distant pat-pat of running
feet, she hardly knew, the sound was so faint and far away at first.
She stopped that she might give full attention to listening for a
moment. The sound now became more distinct. Su-lan peered back
into the darkness from which the sound came. She could see nothing; so she walked on from one lamp to another, stopping at intervals
to listen. Now the steps could be heard distinctly. She flattened
herself against the dark shelter of a pillar beside one of the gateways
halfway between two of the street lamps.

Two coolies pulling empty rickshas and chattering to each other
appeared out of the darkness. They came opposite to where Su-lan
waited hardly daring to breathe. But the men went on. The sound
of their voices and their footsteps faded away into silence, and they
disappeared.

The child heaved a sigh and continued in the same general
direction until finally she arrived at the wide avenue, Ch'ien Men
Street. There was no question now about which way to go. This
broad avenue led directly north to the Front Gate of the city. No
more was she a solitary figure on a lonely street. Now occasional
carriages and rickshas passed by. The light traffic made her less
conspicuous. Now and then an automobile bearing officials home
from theaters or late parties passed, causing the other traffic to give
way.

Su-lan felt some of the old spirit of freedom well up in her. She
kept to the edge of the wide avenue, and stopped now and then to

look at the shop windows, which were not boarded up in this part of the city. Distributors of furs and silks and silver had their places of business on this and nearby streets. Su-lan noted the signs and the window displays. This was even more fascinating than Lantern Street. But it was not as she had expected. It was not like the vicinity of the wall near her home. Here was no moat; here were no refugee shacks. The moat had been drained and filled with soil and leveled off to make a roadbed for the railroad lines coming into the northern capital. Su-lan remembered hearing talk about the noisy *hwah cheh* (fire carts). She had heard how the quiet waters of the canal in some sections of the city no more carried pleasure barges in the summer nor iceboats in the winter. The talk had been about the railroads made for the fire carts. She had heard that the Manchu court had refused to allow the railroads to come into the city proper so that the terminal had been built outside the Tartar City.

Su-lan gazed at the square, solidly built station that seemed oddly out of place by the curving triple roofs of the giant Front Gate nearby. The gate loomed up dark and forbidding against the backdrop of the pale light from the city beyond. The gate's eight-story tower loomed up greater and more majestic than the North Gate tower on the opposite side of the city. This looked mountainous to the wondering eye of Su-lan as she came closer to it.

The closer she came, the more she realized that she would not find here what she had expected, a good place to hide. A wide highway with heavy traffic streamed under the arch of the lofty tower. She looked around for the small buildings or deserted shacks she had expected to find. Now it seemed that she had come to the end of her plans.

But a wide plaza spread out before the gate and over to the large square gray building where many people went in and out and rickshas kept coming and going.

Su-lan walked over and mingled with the crowd outside the building. She noted that no doorman stood at the door. People went in and came out freely. At last she herself decided to go in.

Inside were long rows of seats. Every seat seemed to be filled even at this still early hour of the morning. A number of weary-looking travelers squatted on the floor. Here a man slept, stretched out full-length on the floor, with only a handkerchief shielding his head from the cold pavement. There a woman huddled in the corner with two children lying on the floor on either side of her with their heads resting in her lap. The woman clutched a baby in her arms.

No one paid the slightest attention to Su-lan; so she walked around. This certainly was a fascinating place. One small room contained a strange window with bars. A man stayed in the small room and talked to people who came up to him. In another room Su-lan saw rows of shelves with baskets and cases on the shelves. There were various exits and side rooms too. Su-lan went out one of the doors.

"Why, this must be the fire cart station." She had never seen a train, as her entire life had been spent on the other side of the city except for the few months she had been at Madam Fan's place. But she remembered everything she had heard about the fire carts. Possibly if she waited long enough in this place she might see one come in.

The longer she stayed at the station and mingled with the people, the more at home Su-lan felt. Perhaps here she would be less easily discovered than at any other place. Just how long she could hide here or where she would go next she had no idea, but right now it seemed the best place to be. She would be in no hurry to find another place, she decided.

A Strange Place to Hide

Su-lan looked all around the station before deciding where would be the best place to squeeze in. Finally she chose a spot near a family with small children. Here she felt she would not be conspicuous. The three small children lay asleep on quilts spread out on the floor. Su-lan sat down beside the parents, who barely glanced up at her. Only when some of the queer white-faced foreigners passed through the waiting room, or there were some sharp words between travelers and coolies over the matter of payment, did the parents seem to pay attention to anything.

The space, just big enough for Su-lan to squeeze into, gave her a feeling of being well-hidden and inconspicuous as if she had already arrived in some far-distant city. She took off her shawl and placed it on the floor to sit on, and as she did she noticed something tied in one corner. Quickly she untied it. Wrapped in a dried lotus leaf she found some rolls of steamed bread which Goh Amah must have hidden in the shawl for her, and in her excitement she had not noticed.

While walking through the dark streets, Su-lan had had no time to think of her hunger, but now, warm and comfortable, and able to relax for a time, she felt ravenous. She knew she should save one of the *man-tou* for tomorrow; but when she had tasted the good wheaty flavor, savory with a smear of salted cabbage, she knew that tomorrow would have to take care of itself, and she finished every morsel. Then she leaned back and thought gratefully of Goh Amah and dreamed of the time when she might repay the old woman for her many little favors.

Su-lan, unlike many of the weary people in the station, watched all that went on around her. The coming and going of people, the meetings of friends and loved ones, and the handling of baggage all interested her. Absorbed in watching, she gradually leaned against the person next to her and at last fell fast asleep.

When she awoke, she rubbed her eyes. Where was she? Slowly she remembered the events of the night and early morning. Certainly she had not meant to sleep in this public place. And what about Fan Tai Tai? Had she begun her search yet? Would the police come in here?

Then she saw them. Police around the railway terminus! Several of them stood at that very moment outside one of the doors. They wore khaki uniforms, and their rifles hung over their shoulders. They seemed to be chatting happily together as if not very much impressed with their duties.

The family who had been next to Su-lan had left. On one side a well-dressed woman sat. Her two little boys, in long padded robes reaching to the feet, with stout padded trousers neatly tied at the ankles and showing beneath their robes, arranged their pieces of baggage to form a playhouse. They laughed and jumped about, happy in their play. Their mother sat cross-legged on the floor, placidly sewing on a shoe sole.

"I must decide on a plan," Su-lan thought. "I cannot remain here for too long. I may be able to bluff along for a few days as a member of one of these families." But she knew that the longer she stayed, the more likely she would be to attract notice. If the police were searching for her, she could hardly escape attention if she continued to remain in any one spot.

Su-lan considered what she might do. She had seen others, when the trains pulled out, squeeze into the crowd on the steps and stow away. She could do it if she tried, and a train ride would be an exciting experience! But this plan would not really help very much. She would still be hungry, and she wouldn't know what to do when she got off the train, wherever that might be.

Perhaps she could offer her services as a nursemaid to one of these families with children. But who would accept such help from a total stranger? She looked down at her ragged clothes and dirty hands. She touched her hair. It had not been combed since her imprisonment. Her most urgent need for the moment was to see

what she could do to clean herself up. She made her way to the
restroom and washed her hands and face as best she could without
soap or a towel. She felt in her pocket for her little wooden comb.
It was still there. Painfully she tried to pull the comb through her
blood-matted hair. It had been neglected ever since Madam Fan
had pushed her into the prison room after beating her. But Su-lan
smoothed it as best she could and went back to the waiting room.

When she returned, her place had been taken. But at the end
of one of the long seats a man arose and left. Su-lan quickly slipped
into his place. So intent was she on finding a place to sit that she
did not notice the person beside whom she sat. With a start she
noticed the man was not Chinese, but a foreigner.

This one had a newspaper from which he appeared to be reading.
He must be quite old, Su-lan thought, for he wore a short beard on
his chin and a stubby mustache on his upper lip. But his face did not
look old. He had a ruddy but smooth complexion with deep creases
at his mouth. His hair was the color of rice straw.

Could this foreigner be the same one that Pear Blossom had told
them about in Madam Fan's kitchen? Although most foreigners
looked much alike, not many wore either beard or moustache. The
more she thought of what Pear Blossom had said about the man, the
more she stared and became convinced that this must be the same
man.

Not that it made any difference, but she did want to know if he
had been the one to order the lantern from Fan Tai Tai's shop. She
remembered about the gold watch. Did all foreigners carry gold
watches?

After thinking about this for some time, she decided to find out.

"Honorable old man," she addressed him in the polite form, "can
you tell me what time it is?" She hoped she sounded as if it were
a common thing for her to talk to strange foreigners.

The man looked down at her. She noticed his eyes, deep set and
blue. They seemed to see right through her. She wished she could
hide her worn jacket and tattered shoes.

For a moment she thought he would not speak. Then in excellent
Chinese he answered, "Certainly."

Reaching inside his coat, he drew out a large gold watch and
turned it slightly toward her. "It is just eleven o'clock."

Su-lan's eyes glowed as she looked at the watch. Her plan had worked. This must be the man who had come to the lantern shop. Now she watched as he slipped the watch back into his pocket and went back to reading the newspaper.

He must have lived in China for a long time, Su-lan decided. He spoke the language as well as a Chinese. She would like to talk more with him. Every now and again he looked away from his paper and down at her. Was he curious about her as she was about him?

The man laid down his paper, and Su-lan felt his eyes on her.

Then the man looked up at the wall at the far end of the room. A large clock hung on the wall, plainly visible to all. He looked down rather sharply then. He patted his pocket where he no doubt had his wallet. He probably thought she was a pickpocket. Then he asked her pointblank, "Are you waiting for the train?"

"No," she replied. "I'm looking for a job."

"Eh? What? You're looking for a job? What do you mean?" he exclaimed.

"This is true talk." She looked up at him. "Do you know of anyone who could use a *ku-niang* to help take care of their children?"

The man laughed. "I suppose you have a long list of recommendations? Is this some kind of joke? You are sitting in the railroad station all alone. You ask what time it is, but you are looking for a job?"

"I just wanted to see your watch. Pear Blossom told me about it, and I had never seen one. I'm sorry, I didn't mean any harm."

"Now, wait a minute. Who in thunder is Pear Blossom?"

"One of the girls at Madam Fan's," Su-lan answered. "She was in the Lantern Shop when you came to buy a lantern; she told us about you in the kitchen. Aren't you the one who ordered a lantern?"

"This joke gets better and better," the man said. And he seemed to be enjoying himself. "You mean, little girl, that only one person bought a lantern at Fan Tai Tai's, and that I'm the one?"

"Oh, no, I didn't mean that. But Pear Blossom told us about only one *wai-kuo-jen* and he had a—" Su-lan looked at the man's stubby beard and moustache and hesitated to repeat the identifying description.

"I think I understand that part of it now. But if you come from Fan Tai Tai's, what are you doing over here?"

5—H.F.S.

Su-lan looked around to see if anyone else was listening to their conversation. Apparently the people next to them were not paying any attention.

"She beat me, and I ran away." She spoke so low he could hardly hear her.

Stanley Brown looked down at the child beside him.

Every day he met dozens of crying, moaning beggars with outstretched arms calling him "Lao Yeh, Lao Yeh [Venerable old man]," and they persistently paced beside his ricksha while he ignored them and looked straight ahead. He knew them for the racket they were in and never gave them a second thought. He was familiar with misery in the form of famine refugees and the maimed and mutilated specimens of humanity which are never absent from the streets of China. He was accustomed to them, and he had long since reconciled himself to the idea that since he couldn't help them all, personally, why let any of them get under his skin?

He knew how to ward off less obvious appeals for help, and he had always been able to steel himself against the efforts on the part of friends or relatives of some other Chinese friend to gain his assistance for some needy person. Why, one could not live in China if he didn't turn a deaf ear to these things. There were so many frauds and schemers to look out for.

"So? Well, I hope you find your job," Mr. Brown said. "But quite probably, you know, you'll have to go back to Fan Tai Tai." He folded up his paper and arose to go.

As he walked away he couldn't help but wonder about the child. What relation did she have to Fan Tai Tai? How long did she think she could hold out by herself in a station? What was she doing for food? Impatiently he put these thoughts out of his mind as he left the station. But she was such a game little thing. Not whining, or asking for help, or beating around the bush. Someone would probably find her and take her back to her aunt, or whoever Fan Tai Tai was. Children were always running away from home and thinking they were mistreated. "She beat me, and I ran away." He could not forget the matter-of-fact yet tragic way that the child had said the words. But probably what she called a beating had just been a light rapping. The girl had a high spirit and wouldn't stand for a real beating.

A Visit to the Lantern Shop

Peking had been the seat of China's government for hundreds of years. So long in fact, that it would seem that by now the affairs of state would be somewhat settled. But even though the empire had changed to a republican form of government, still there had been continual unrest and changes in office. Every few years a great political upheaval upset the old government and a new leader took over the presidential mansion.

These affairs were upsetting. They were upsetting to schoolboys who had to learn the names of the cabinet members so often. They were upsetting to those few whose rank and fortunes were so suddenly shifted from the top to the bottom because of the upheavals. They were upsetting to the stationers and merchants who had recently sent complimentary samples of their stocks to the newly "elected" officers. They were upsetting to train schedules, for such a change always involved a great deal of activity and bustle and moving of troops in and out of the capital. But life in general in the ancient capital was no more upset by these events than the depths of the ocean are disturbed by a squall on the surface, or a giant redwood by a few weeks of drought.

Stanley Brown was never disturbed by them. In ten years of residence in Peking he had seen governments rise and fall, heads lopped off right and left, figuratively speaking. It meant nothing to him beyond affording more interesting news dispatches to send out. No one worried too much about the government. It had very little to do, at that time, with the way of life of the people who followed their own ways and often did not even know who the president was.

It would take more than a change of government to shake the fixed pattern of Stanley Brown's days. He lived alone and liked it. That is, if living in the almost constant presence of Kuei-bin, his Number One houseboy, could be called living alone. Kuei-bin acted also as butler, cook, wash boy, and table waiter.

Every morning at seven Kuei-bin opened the door of Mr. Brown's bedroom and came in with the morning paper and a cup of hot tea, and very pleasantly remarked about the fine "heavenly atmosphere" and added that Mr. Brown's "wash-all-over" was prepared, and that "early rice" would be ready in half an hour. Having thus fulfilled the requirement of etiquette, he would stay and chat informally for a while. Kuei-bin was an almanac, a gossip sheet, and a newscaster all in one. Stanley Brown liked him, and Kuei-bin knew it. No houseboy could have been better suited to his peculiar needs if the boy had been ordered from a mail-order catalogue. A perfectionist who managed the small domain of his master's house with easy skill, Kuei-bin tried to manage his master as well. This, Stanley Brown let him think he did.

Kuei-bin enjoyed good pay and not too heavy duties. From time to time he thought wistfully of larger households where the Number One boy had more power, and more specialized work, and where there were more interesting incidents to report to his friends. But the freedom from a heavy program of entertaining with its extra responsibilities and late hours compensated for them.

Stanley Brown rarely entertained, but on the other hand he frequently dined out. His work as a newspaper correspondent took him away from home a great deal, and when at home, he felt like a man in his castle, enjoying a book, free from interruption.

A womanless household quite satisfied both Kuei-bin and his master. Kuei-bin had the run of the house with full responsibility and no interference. Stanley Brown had found China the ideal place for a bachelor existence, for his daily needs were taken care of without either great expense or much attention on his part.

About twice a year he visited his sister, Florence, and her family in Shanghai. After a week with his sister and four small nieces, the return to his own home was like a retreat to a monastery.

But he did like people. On the train, in the market, on the street, in all his contacts, he saw people as individuals; and even in brief contacts at the market or in the shops he always tried to learn more about the lives of those around him. He laughed with them and joked with them and jollied them along.

His efforts to joke with Kuei-bin usually fell flat, for Kuei-bin had little sense of humor, and besides he had a dignity to maintain. "You surely must have been a hard drinker in your day," Stanley would say, "to get a red nose like that."

Kuei-bin had told him repeatedly that his red nose had been the result of frostbite, but Stanley Brown couldn't remember. Or if he did, he enjoyed the joke.

"Better put a mitten on that nose tonight," he would say. "It's going to be cold."

Kuei-bin ignored such pleasantries, sometimes allowing the slightest upward curl of his lips as if amused at the antics of a child.

The next morning after Stanley Brown had talked with the child in the station, Kuei-bin entered his master's bedroom as usual bringing a tray with a pot of steaming tea, and the morning paper. He shut the window and adjusted the blinds.

"Gooda morning," he said, using all the English he knew.

Stanley Brown had never found in Chinese any equivalent of the pleasant "good morning." Then both men resorted to Chinese.

"What's news today?" the older man asked, a part of the daily routine. "Any cabinet members resigned? Has General Wu brought his armies any closer to the Fengtai Railroad?" He did not expect Kuei-bin to know the answers to any of these questions, but often Kuei-bin actually did have valuable leads to news items. He read the Chinese newspapers, and by grapevine he picked up a wide variety of news.

"It's a beautiful clear day outside, Hsien Sheng [Master]. Nice day for a trip. I hear that Chang's men are massed along the Great Wall near Chinwang Tao. Also a bridge has been blown up on the Fengtai Railroad. In city, nothing much happen. Everything peaceful. No student riots."

He turned to go out. "The 'wash-all-over,' it is ready. Also, breakfast will be ready when you come down. This morning, very good breakfast, Hsien Sheng."

At the door he stopped. "Oh, Hsien Sheng, what store you buy your new lampshade—the big one with carved dragon stand?"

"Why, at Fan Tai Tai's, outside in the Chinese City. Why?"

"Oh, nothing. Nothing important. Just wondered. Fan Tai Tai, she advertise in Chinese paper today for little girl named Su-lan. Say she kidnapped. Reward."

Kuei-bin had the habit of reporting many trivial bits of hearsay along with some things of greater importance. He never knew when he might pass on something which would be of value to his master. His almond eyes narrowed as he watched to see what reaction, if any, this bit of news might bring.

"So what?" Stanley Brown said jokingly, giving no inkling that he gave a second thought to any of Kuei-bin's reports. "Maybe you can find out by grapevine where she is and claim the reward!"

So, her name was Su-lan. The small appealing face and her last words, "She beat me, and I ran away," came into Brown's mind. He wondered what the relation was between the girl and the owner of the lantern shop. If Madam Fan offered a reward for her, there was not much chance but that she would be found eventually.

"It means nothing at all to me." Kuei-bin shrugged and went out to attend to his preparation for breakfast.

"It means nothing at all to me either," Stanley Brown said to himself. But for some strange reason his mind kept returning to the incident of the day before. "Can't let this get under my skin," he thought. "Why, if one got to worrying about all the needy youngsters around him in China, he'd never have a moment's contentment."

Oh, there had been times when people had come to him for aid, and he had been positively convinced of the need. He had gone all-out to help. He could even ignore Kuei-bin, who could make his disapproval quite unpleasant if he wanted to.

Mr. Brown remembered the time when a young Russian had come to his door, ragged and dirty and unshaven. He had said he'd been months on the road on foot, in an incredible trek from Siberia where he had been sent as a prisoner for preaching the gospel. He had no recommendations, no proof other than his own word that his story was true.

But Stanley Brown, sure of his own ability to judge people, had taken him in, given him clean clothing and a bath and his guest room. He had housed him for two weeks until the man had rested and could continue his journey to his hoped-for destination—America. He had even helped make the necessary arrangements for the Russian to contact those of his church who could help him with a passport and funds.

As Stanley Brown started out in his ricksha this day, he again thought of the strange little girl and her friendly, plucky spirit. He hated to admit any interest in her problem, but since Kuei-bin had told him of the newspaper item, he thought of the strange coincidence that he had seen this same little girl the day before. It surely must be the same little girl. Strange how she had talked about his having been in the Lantern Shop! And she had been so positive about her not returning there. For some strange reason Stanley Brown directed his ricksha to Lantern Street.

Fan Tai Tai had not been in the shop when he had ordered his lantern that day just before the New Year. Her shop had been highly recommended to him as one of the best. She must be an able businesswoman. He intended to see this woman.

He had no intention of ordering another lantern when he went into the shop. Even though he knew that the bargaining skill of a thousand generations would be pitted against his resistance, yet he determined to "look-see" without buying anything.

Lan, the dapper young man who had waited on Stanley Brown before, bowed low. He apparently remembered this foreigner with the bristling moustache and plenty of money, and he greeted him with a toothy smile. Lan expressed warm affection while trying to assure the customer that he would be happy to sell him unlimited numbers of expensive lanterns.

"Have many very beautiful new lampshades. All color, all shape," Lan said, waving his hand in a wide gesture around the shop. "You want look-see? No hurry. Plenty time. What kind you want?"

"I'm pretty sure you don't have just what I want," Stanley Brown said truthfully. "But I'd like to look around for a few minutes if you don't mind. My sister in Shanghai would like a lampshade from Peking, but she has a very definite notion of what she wants. You know how women are. It must go with drapes, rugs, certain colors, certain style, et cetera."

"Oh, yes, I know, I know, Hsien Sheng tell what color, what shape, how big, and we make him. Make very good. You like."

Stanley Brown thought for a minute. He tried to remember what Florence's living room was like, and at the same time to think of something to ask for that they wouldn't have in the shop. He could always say he couldn't wait to have anything made. He would like to think of some excuse to ask for Fan Tai Tai, or possibly if he delayed a few minutes, she might come into the shop.

"I'm not sure I want to wait to have something made," he said at last. "Do you have something that would go in a European-style room? I think probably late Victorian would be about right." He tried not to smile at the puzzled look that came over Lan's face.

"Late—Victorian— What you mean?"

Stanley Brown made another stab. "Oh, something in rose silk with a lot of ruffles, shaped something like an umbrella, you know. Say, it's hard to describe. I'll just look around and see if you have anything like that." He knew he wouldn't find a monstrosity such as he had described in any Chinese shop.

Lan turned to look over his lanterns. He brought out a few of his creations like a clerk in a dress shop bringing forth dresses for customers to try on. But his delicate works of art, transparent silk painted in picture stories stretched over a framework of light bamboo, did not suit Stanley Brown at all.

"Now look here. A store with a name like yours, 'Righteous, Virtuous, International Lantern Shop,' should make a stronger effort to please all tastes." Stanley Brown reproached Lan. "Why don't you put in a stock of lamps suitable for European homes? Don't you know there are a large number of foreigners in Peking now who would probably buy them if you had them?"

Lan bowed politely, agreeing with his customer. *"Dwei-la! Dwei-la!* [Right! Right!] Wait just a minute, I'll be right out." He stepped to the door and returned in a moment.   .

Lan withdrew to the rear of the room. Out of the corner of his eye Stanley Brown saw him busying himself replacing his stocks, like a general withdrawing from the field.

And then a woman, the picture of poise and competence, perfectly groomed in a long black gown with a trim of red-gold braid on neck and sleeve bands, stepped up to Stanley Brown.

"What kind of lamp do you wish?" She spoke with a low compelling voice. "I am sure that we have something to please you."

"I am very sorry to have troubled you. It is of no importance whatever," Mr. Brown replied truthfully. "I would like to send my sister in Shanghai a gift from your shop, but I don't find what I am looking for. Of course, I should not expect to find an English shade in a Chinese shop." He turned toward the door.

"Many English people buy our shades. We have styles and colors to suit all tastes."

She brought out a masterpiece of ornate design, octagonal in shape with a long black tassel hanging at the apex. "This is one which English people like very much. See, there are several colors on a neutral background, and it would be suitable for any room. Is it not beautiful? Would you like me to ship it direct, or will you take it with you?"

This woman must be Fan Tai Tai, Stanley Brown mused. He observed the hard cold eyes, and guessed at the firmness and ruthlessness with which she might deal with those under her authority. Now he thought of the child. What was this woman to Su-lan? he wondered. Judging by the child's garb, he could come to only one conclusion.

"Thank you," he decided quickly, "but it is not what I want." He spoke positively and turned out the door. But not without noticing from the corner of his eye the fixed steady glance which said that Fan Tai Tai would not forget this customer.

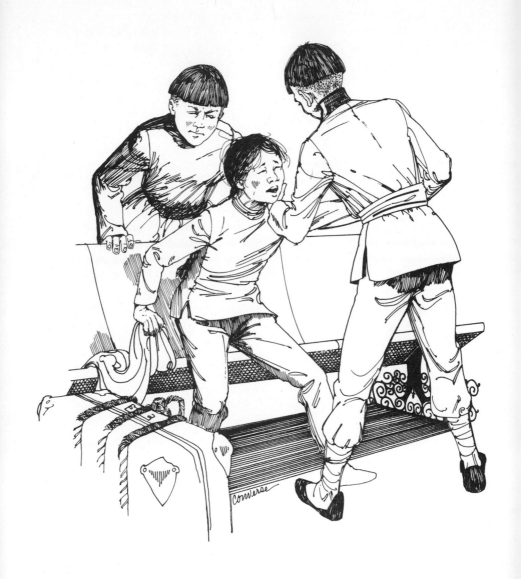

Never Talk to Strangers

By the afternoon of the second day after Su-lan's escape, she felt as much at home in the railroad station as she had been in the lanes and courts of Fried Fish Alley near her father's house. She knew every entrance and exit, every seat and bench and ticket window. She had tried out a number of different places to sit which gave her views of people going to the trains or coming from them; she had seen people elaborately dressed in furs and silks, moving to the trains amid a flutter of servants and coolies or coming from them with birdcages and ice-cream freezers in hand. But the queer foreigners who came into the station and who wore their fur coats wrong side out, and had the most foolish-looking hats atilt sideways on their heads, amused her no end.

She had made brief acquaintances with several Chinese among the patient throng of those waiting for trains. One Chinese mother surrounded by little ones had seemed grateful when Su-lan offered to hold the baby, as round as a ball in his padded jackets and trousers. The mother handed her a few coppers when they left for their train.

What luck! With this money she could buy a few fried cakes from one of the many vendors who crowded the railway platform at train time. She chewed the salty, savory fried cakes slowly, thoughtfully, making each morsel linger as long in her mouth as possible—enjoying the crisp, greasy crunch, and the flavor of the peanut oil.

Having eaten a little, she enjoyed all the more the novel sights and sounds around her.

The arrival of the "fire carts" with their ferocious black engines, clanging and puffing and hissing like monster dragons, terrified but fascinated her. They came to a stop with a terrific jolt as if a convulsion passed over the dragon, jerking the doors open and shaking out the people.

The crowds came and went. Only the people waiting to depart remained any length of time in the station. And who was there among them to take any notice of those who came or those who went, or to observe one small girl who never bought a ticket or showed herself too close to the men punching tickets?

In general, the people in the crowds paid little attention to each other, taking for granted the differences of dress and station in life. But the minute one of the white foreigners, whether man, woman, or child, made an appearance, the eyes of all were turned toward him with curious stares.

In the afternoon a young foreign woman carrying a small child came in and sat down on her baggage while her husband bought tickets and arranged for the checking of the larger pieces of luggage. The children in the room came over to have a good look at the strange fair child. Mothers followed, and soon a compact ring stood around the woman and her child, watching.

Su-lan pressed in among them, not wanting to miss anything of interest. She thought of the day on the moat and the smiles and laughter of the young couple putting on their skates. But she saw at once that this white-faced woman with the red lips looked alarmed and frightened, and held her baby close to her. Su-lan noticed that some of the women patted the baby's hands and felt of its clothes.

If only the white woman could understand, she would not be frightened, Su-lan thought. These people are only curious.

"A German, I think," said one of the crowd.

"Oh, no, Russian most surely," said another.

"Idiot, stupid cow. American, if there ever was one. Only Americans are thin and undernourished like that."

One of the women poked the young mother with a bony finger, and pointed at the baby. "How many months?" she asked.

The foreign woman didn't answer, but looked more frightened than ever as if she thought they intended to snatch the child away. Tears filled her eyes.

The crowd stared unfeelingly. *"Bu dung,"* one said, and then the others repeated the words. *"Ta bu dung.* [She doesn't understand us]."

The comments continued, and the crowd thickened. Su-lan alone, it seemed, sensed the distress felt by this stranger from a far-away land who could not talk their language.

Impulsively she turned and spoke a few words in a positive voice to those nearest to her. Someone repeated the words, and, as if by magic, the mothers grabbed their children and got away as suddenly as if the victim of their curiosity had turned into a mad dog.

The husband of the woman returned just then with the tickets and the coolies, and he quickly got rid of the rest of the crowd with a few angry words and gestures.

Su-lan noticed the look of relief on the woman's face as she clung to her husband's arm. "Oh, I'm so glad you came just now. I thought I was going to faint with all those horrible staring eyes upon me. But that little girl said something that made them go. I wonder what it was. Did you hear?"

"I didn't hear what *she* said," the husband laughed, "but I can guess what it was from what I heard some others say. Evidently she told those people that Linda had the cholera and you were just trying to get her to the hospital."

Su-lan had acted on impulse, without thinking of what the consequences might be. Her natural tendency to push her way to the front had made her forget to be cautious for the moment. She had really been enjoying her life in the station enough to make her forget a little the concern she had felt about being returned to Madam Fan. She had thought herself free from observation and had mingled with the crowds almost forgetting the punishment room at Madam Fan's and her days of rough work.

But now she noticed over in the far corner of the station two gangly youths, dressed in the faded uniforms of some school. Whenever Su-lan looked their way, they seemed to be looking at her. Then they would look away quickly or begin to read the newspaper.

After a few moments Su-lan saw them look her way again. Then one of the boys whispered to the other.

"I say, Hung, she could be the one," the taller of the two boys said quietly to his companion. "She's the right age, and the clothes answer to the description."

"But that's no proof." Hung cupped his hands around his mouth as he tried to light a cigarette butt he had picked up off the floor. "Any one of a thousand girls would answer the same description. 'Blue cotton jacket and worn gray padded trousers.' Wonder why they couldn't think of something better to identify her."

"It would have been a help. But you know, there is something strange about that girl over there. She isn't with anyone. She doesn't seem to be waiting for a train. She must be the one. I'll wager two silver dimes, big money."

"Sure, Lo, but we can't claim a reward on a hunch. There must be some way to find out." Hung spoke through a cloud of smoke.

"Step right up and ask her, brother. I am sure she would tell you," the older boy said sarcastically.

"If we could get to talking with her, we might find out enough. I have an idea. We could call her by her name. If it is Su-lan, she would probably show it."

"Suppose we do decide she's the one, what's the next step?"

"You shadow her, while I take a ricksha out to the address given in the ad in the paper."

The boys sauntered over by Su-lan.

After a little while, when another train had come and gone and the people who had been sitting near Su-lan left, the two crowded into the vacant space.

They talked in loud voices to each other, complaining about the irregularity of the train service and blaming the government for allowing such a state of affairs. As they spoke they watched the girl out of the corner of their eyes.

At last one of the boys turned to Su-lan. "Been waiting long?" he asked casually.

Su-lan turned and looked full at him, unsmiling. She hesitated just a moment before answering. "Yes, quite a while."

"Where are you going?" the other boy asked.

"I'm not going anywhere," she admitted frankly.

The boys winked at each other.

"I'm waiting to meet someone," she invented cheerfully.

After a few minutes Su-lan rose to go to another part of the room.

"Su-lan!" the one boy said sharply, "you'd better stay here!"

Su-lan jumped.

"Sit down again, Su-lan," the boy commanded. "Do just what we tell you, and you'll be all right. But I am warning you, if you make the slightest disturbance, we will call the police."

She sat down. The boy took hold of her arm, gripping it with hard, wiry fingers. "So, you thought you'd have a little vacation and see the world, did you? Well, it's all over now, and you're going back to Fan Tai Tai's."

"I'll go out and arrange with the ricksha pullers," the one called Lo directed. "You and the girl follow in just a few minutes. Walk out like a good little Mei Mei," he said to Su-lan, "and my friend here will not have to twist your arm." The fellow hurried out of the building.

After some minutes had passed, her captor gave her a gentle shove. She walked along ahead of him, but her mind frantically grasped at ideas of how to escape. No one seemed to pay attention as Su-lan and her captor walked across the room and toward the door. The child looked this way and that, casting about for someone to help her. But she did not dare to cry out or call attention to herself, nor did she know that her captors had no interest in getting help from the police, or causing any commotion that might result in an investigation. Their interest was to return her to Fan Tai Tai so they could collect the reward.

Now the massive waiting-room door closed behind Su-lan and her captor. There stood the other boy with three rickshas. The rickshas and their pullers were apart from the others; so the girl knew the boy had made the arrangements. There would be no haggling over prices. There would be no time for her to call attention to herself or these boys. Roughly they pushed her toward one of the rickshas.

Terror gripped Su-lan. Was there no one to help a—

At that moment a tall foreigner stepped from a ricksha that pulled up near the station. Su-lan saw his ruddy face and the bristling sandy moustache and short clipped beard. She gave a sudden jerk of her arm and loosed herself from the boy's grasp. But he reached out and grabbed her before she moved away.

But Su-lan saw the tall foreigner striding over.

"Here, here! What's going on?" he demanded, looking from one to the other of the boys.

"She's our sister, and we are just taking her home, *Hsien Sheng*. She's a lazy good-for-nothing and likes to wander on the streets or in the market instead of staying at home and doing her work like a proper girl should," the one boy said. "You cannot imagine how much trouble—"

But the foreigner raised his hand to silence him. "Save yourself the trouble of thinking up any more. She isn't your sister, and you know it. Besides, I know who she is. I'm taking care of her. Now, *chu-ba*," he waved his hand, "both of you."

He turned to Su-lan. "Come. Get into the ricksha. You're coming home with me."

For the third time in her life Su-lan rode in a ricksha. This time she did not slump in the seat. She sat up straight, considering everything around her. Only once did she think of her first ride and her father padding rhythmically along on the pavement in front of her on that day so long ago. How long had it been?

She had no idea where this foreigner was taking her or what he intended to do with her. But he had taken matters into his own hands, and Su-lan trusted him. Everything from now on would be all right. She smiled and nodded to the foreigner as he turned and their eyes met.

Through the Moon Door

Although Su-lan had no concern about what would happen to her, her companion in the other ricksha did not share her peace of mind.

"What will I do with the little hoodlum?" he mulled over in his mind. He had to face Kuei-bin. What would he have to say? Kuei-bin would certainly question his good judgment. Of course he wouldn't come right out and say so. Nothing, no, nothing, could startle that one's outward calm or alter his dignified manner. The respectable houseboy doubtless would not show any surprise if his master should return home sometime with a couple of pandas in his arms and say, "See my new pets? Find a place for them."

Stanley Brown shrugged. No, Kuei-bin would probably say nothing. He would do the thing expected of him in his usual cheerful manner. It had never mattered what the unusual thing might be. Extra washing, extra dishes, even disagreeable tasks that did not ordinarily fall to his lot. But some time later, after a week, or two, or more, Kuei-bin's grandmother would die, or some distant cousin would meet disaster, and Kuei-bin would go. He might come back, and he might not. So far, he had. Stanley Brown wondered if he had any more grandmothers to die.

This roundabout method of meeting problems exasperated Stanley Brown. One couldn't argue with a dead grandmother. One couldn't infer by so much as a look that the story was doubted. One couldn't ask what was the matter, or offer to make amends if there were any grievances.

How much better, he thought, it would be if he could just talk things over frankly with Kuei-bin, each saying what he really

81

thought, and then each adjust himself to the other's ideas if necessary. These thoughts twisted and turned in his mind while the coolies trotted down the road pulling the rickshas.

Now they passed through the legation quarters where the representatives of all the foreign governments had their residences. And while Stanley Brown mulled over his problem, Su-lan's eyes darted from one substantial square stone building to another. Never had she seen anything like this before.

The coolies continued north and then turned west. Finally they entered a narrow *hutung* with high walls on either side. They let down their shafts before a well-kept gate with freshly painted red doors. Stanley Brown counted out the money for the ricksha pullers; then he turned to Su-lan.

"Well, here we are, my little runaway. Now, I don't know what to do with you next." He lifted the ponderous latch, and they went in.

In the courtyard they had entered, paved with smooth flat stones and decorated with potted plants, Su-lan stood transfixed. A round open door at one side of the courtyard invited into another, and a winding pebbled pathway led to the house.

"What's the matter? Don't you like my insignificant dwelling?"

"Oh, but it is beautiful!" the little girl exclaimed. "A two-story house. I have never been in a two-story house before."

"You'll be seeing a lot of strange things," Stanley Brown said in an undertone. "You are a real little extrovert," he added aloud, and his laughter caused Su-lan to look up into his face.

"It is sort of fun to show things to one who has eyes to see, and a heart to admire and wonder, and to one who is not afraid to comment." He saw the puzzled look on Su-lan's face, but before either spoke again the door opened, and there stood Kuei-bin. His impassive face showed no interest or surprise at the sight of the tattered little stranger. He stood at the door in his long white gown buttoned at the sides, his shoes of smooth black satin, and his stockings of pure white with white tie cloths. There was not the slightest flicker of an eyelash.

"This little girl had some trouble over at the station, so I—well —I—just brought her home for a few days," Stanley Brown said. Why did he have to explain this to his servant?

"I will keep her until I can find someone to take care of her," he added. "Fix the guest room so she can sleep there tonight, and set another place at the table. I'm sure she can do with a little food."

Kuei-bin nodded. "Dinner will be ready in a few minutes, *Hsien Sheng.*"

Now why had he suggested that she eat at the same table with him? Stanley Brown frowned. He should have had her eat in the kitchen. Not with Kuei-bin, of course, for the cook ate his meals in his own quarters—he loathed American foods.

Then, looking down at Su-lan's rapt expression as she gazed around the room, he laughed softly. How would this one get along with a knife, fork, and spoon, and a plateful of potatoes, roast, and vegetables?

But Su-lan seemed to have no thought of food just then. Stanley Brown watched her as she took in the soft rugs on the floor, the cases of books, the elegant furniture, the pictures, and the draperies.

"Come!" Stanley Brown interrupted her thoughts. "I'm sure you'll want to wash up before you eat." He started down the hall, and Su-lan followed.

"This is the bathroom. Here is a towel and a washcloth." Then turning on the faucets he showed her the one with the hot water and the one with the cold. "You may lock the door if you like," he added. "Take your time." He left Su-lan standing in the middle of the mirrored room.

Alone in the room, Su-lan slipped the bolt in the lock. She ran her fingers over the smooth cold whiteness of the bathtub. Never had she seen such a toilet or washbasin with running water! She tried all the knobs and handles and faucets to see how they worked.

Looking up, she saw her reflection in the mirror, a grimy, untidy little girl. She grimaced. Then, turning on the faucet, she filled the basin with steaming hot water. After removing her jacket, she wrung the towel out of the hot water as best she could without burning her hands. Then she rubbed her face and neck and arms with it.

How dirty the towel became! But she soaped it and washed it out in fresh water.

Then from her jacket pocket she took her tiny comb, the only toilet article she possessed, and after unbraiding her hair she combed it carefully. If only she had some oil to make it shiny. She wet the comb and slicked her hair over her temples again and again until at last it satisfied her. Then she unlocked the door and went out.

In the dining room she found Stanley Brown seated at the table. Su-lan looked at the array of linens, cutlery, and glassware. And there was her new friend watching her. This would be a test to see how she would meet and react to situations. And the girl made up her mind to please. If only she knew what were the right things to do or say!

She fingered the white cloth on the table under the dishes. Instead of a bowl in front of her there was a flat plate and on either side of it strange utensils, but no chopsticks. A small plate on one side and two glasses on the other side of the plate seemed strange. One of the glasses had clear cold water in it and a strange square of something that looked like glass. This must be ice, the kind that foreigners make in their strange white machines, Su-lan thought, remembering something she had heard in Madam Fan's kitchen. The other glass contained something white. This must be milk, she decided, although she did not remember ever having had a glass of it.

"Sit down, child," Mr. Brown motioned her to pull out a chair.

As soon as Su-lan sat down, Kuei-bin entered the room through the swinging doors. He placed a small plate on the larger one before her. There were two small crackers on the plate and a glass of bright red juice. Kuei-bin placed a small plate with crackers and a glass of the red juice in front of Mr. Brown too.

Su-lan watched him take up the glass and drink the juice. He ate the crackers too.

"Aren't you going to eat, child?" he asked Su-lan as she sat with her hands folded in her lap.

She wanted to know what the juice in the glass was, but she hardly dared to ask. She twisted her hands in her lap. Then, gingerly she lifted the glass to her lips and sipped the juice. It tasted cold and rather sour. It was hard not to make a face at the strange taste. The crackers were crisp and salty. Suddenly she felt ravenously hungry. Not since before the day Fan Tai Tai had locked her up had she once been satisfied. Of course, until she had gone to the house on Lantern Street Su-lan had never known what it was to eat to the full. Once more she lifted the glass of juice. This time she drained it.

Kuei-bin took away the small plates with the empty glasses. A plate of rolls and a glass dish containing olives and celery remained on the table. Su-lan recognized the celery, but had never seen olives before. Could it be that this was all there would be to eat?

But Kuei-bin returned with a platter. In the center were pieces of meat covered with gravy, and little white balls with green specks in them bordered the platter.

Su-lan stared at the platter as Kuei-bin stood beside her, offering her the platter.

Surely this whole platter could not be for her. What should she do? After a brief hesitation she picked up the large spoon and fork and took a piece of meat from the platter, placing it on her large plate.

Kuei-bin remained at her side. She looked up to see if his face might show approval, but he stood there expressionless. Su-lan served herself one of the little white balls.

"How I wish I could tell Pear Blossom and Peony about these strange things to eat!" she thought. Then she looked up at her host to find him watching her.

"I don't believe you have told me your name," Mr. Brown remarked.

"My name is Su-lan."

"Is that all? There must be something else," he queried.

"No, that is all." The child looked down at her plate.

"Is Su your father's name?"

"No." Su-lan paused, remembering how she had left her father's home. "No, that is not my father's name. My name is Su-lan. That is all."

Mr. Brown had started to eat. Su-lan picked up one of the strange utensils by her plate and stuck it into a piece of meat as she saw Mr. Brown do. The meat tasted good. But such strange flavors. She watched her host and did everything as he did. Now that she had really started to eat, she went about it intently, cleaning every bit of food from the plate.

Then Kuei-bin returned to the room carrying a plate of triangular shaped pastries.

"I've eaten to the full," Su-lan sighed.

"Oh, come now, you can surely have some apple pie, can't you?"

She watched Mr. Brown lift a generous piece onto his plate. Then he cut off a smaller piece with his fork and put it into his mouth.

Su-lan took a small piece of the pastry and tasted it. "Oh, it is so sweet that I cannot eat another bite," she said.

Mr. Brown got up when he finished eating. Su-lan pushed back her chair, too, and followed him out of the room.

"Come, now," he said, leading the way to the living room, "I want you to sit down here and tell me all about yourself. It will be easier for me to know what to do with you."

He motioned to one of the large overstuffed chairs. Su-lan wondered why all the chairs were arranged so carelessly and were not squared with the wall and in neat order as in Chinese homes. She had an impulse to straighten things out and push the chairs against the wall, but she thought better of it. She sank down in the soft cushion of the chair offered to her.

"Now, then," Mr. Brown said after he seated himself, "tell me how you came to be living at Fan Tai Tai's, why she beat you, and what you planned to do when you left there."

Su-lan's mind began to work quickly. How could she tell anyone that her own father had sold her? She must not "lose face" in the eyes of this foreigner.

"We used to live inside the wall," Su-lan began, visualizing some of the compounds she used to look down upon from her position on the tower. "There were trees in our courtyard and potted plants and a spirit screen. We were so happy! We had plenty to eat, nice clothes to wear, and my father owned a small cloth store. But about two years ago he became very sick, and the doctors wanted more and more money! After a while he couldn't take care of his business, and he had a partner, a dishonest man; and somehow, I don't just know how it all came about, he lost the store and we had to leave our home. Gradually things got worse and worse. Mother had so many mouths to feed, and I thought maybe I could earn some money; so—"

"Didn't your father have some brothers or family who could help you out at a time like this?" Mr. Brown asked discreetly.

Su-lan had not had long enough to think the whole thing through and be prepared for questions Mr. Brown might ask. She hesitated and looked down.

"Look, Su-lan," Mr. Brown said seriously, "there is one thing we might just as well get straight right from the start. I like you. I want to help you. But we must be honest and straight with each other. You know the old proverb, 'He who rides a tiger dares not dismount.' Avoiding the truth is like riding a tiger. The farther you go the more dangerous it becomes and the easier to fall off. So, now, tell me the real truth. You don't need to worry. Besides, maybe the real story is more interesting."

Su-lan saw a twinkle in the man's deep blue eyes. Her pride did not seem so important anymore. Beginning with her life in her parents' home, she told of her fun on the moat, her first encounter with the foreigners, the day she left home, and her life at Fan Tai Tai's until the day she had been caught in the apartment. She told her story with animation and without self-pity. Mr. Brown made only a few comments to help bring out the story and give him clues to Su-lan's disposition and nature. Otherwise he sat quietly and listened.

"I'm glad I happened along at the station just when I did. Now you must go to bed. Tomorrow maybe we can think up a plan. I know you must be tired now. I will show you where you are going to sleep tonight." He showed her to her room and then settled himself in his big chair in his bedroom to read the newspaper. The problem of what to do about Su-lan kept pushing its way to the front of his mind. Why had he taken on such a responsibility? Well, he'd worry about it tomorrow, he decided.

He had not read more than half a column before Kuei-bin slipped quietly in and stood in front of him.

"What is it, Kuei-bin?" he said, putting down his paper.

Kuei-bin never looked directly at his master, but spoke as if talking to someone standing at Mr. Brown's elbow. *"Hsien Sheng,"* he began respectfully, "you need amah? Little girl need amah. You want me find you good amah?"

"Amah!" Mr. Brown snorted. "What do I need an amah for? That little girl is big enough to *be* an amah. Besides—"

Kuei-bin spoke up again. "Little girl have no mother. Little girls always need amah. Amah give little girl bath, make little girl clothes. Comb little girl hair."

"But this is not *my* little girl. I'm not going to keep her here. Tomorrow I will take her to her home or find some place for her. Now go out and leave me alone." He picked up the newspaper again, hoping to put an end to this conversation.

"*Hsien Sheng*, I beg you to forgive me. Please to consider one moment. Ragged little beggar not easy to give away. Amah fix up very good to see. More better."

There seemed some logic in Kuei-bin's suggestion. But Stanley Brown could not believe that all this interest was for Su-lan's benefit. What was behind it all?

"Well, so now I need an amah. And I suppose you know right where to find one waiting. Perhaps you—"

Kuei-bin did not hesitate. "Oh, thank you, thank you, *Hsien Sheng*. Oh, yes, sure, I find you amah. I find very good amah. Tomorrow morning she come." And he turned quickly and padded out of the room.

A Plan Develops

Up in her room in Stanley Brown's home, Su-lan stood still and looked around her. She felt uncomfortable. She had never felt this way before. It was not sickness; but it was almost like sickness and really seemed worse.

Never, never in all her life had she felt so totally alone. Even while in the punishment room she could hear the familiar sounds of the courtyard around her. In the station she had been close to her own people. But here in this room she was all alone. There was nothing familiar. Not one thing.

Her eyes moved in wonder over the clean room, cleaner than any room she had ever slept in. She looked carefully at each piece of the dark polished furniture, the soft figured drapes at the windows, and the bed covered with brown brocaded satin. Su-lan touched the spread lightly, smoothing it with her fingers, but it made her hand seem more rough than before.

"I cannot stay here," she thought. "The *Hsien Sheng* is very kind, but I do not belong here. Tomorrow I will have to make other plans." Maybe Mr. Brown would want to take her back to her own home. She thought of the close, dark little room, the *k'ang*, and her brother and sisters drawing together for warmth. It did not seem so cold and dark as she thought of it. Should she go back?

Su-lan pictured herself going back home. She would be riding in a ricksha, and maybe Mr. Brown would be riding in another one. How surprised Ming-li would be and the sisters and brother. Her mother would not show any surprise, and she might even be sadder than ever. And her father? When Su-lan got this far in her imagining, she felt the old hurt and wounded pride arising. There would be all kinds of questions and explaining. She knew her parents would lose face if they knew she had run away. They might even be afraid that Fan Tai Tai *would* look for her. No, she would not go home. Sometime, maybe later when she became rich. But not now!

Su-lan touched the spread on the bed again. She had never slept in such a bed. She would not do so now. The room was not cold, and she would feel more at home on the floor with her scarf about her. She clung to the one familiar possession in her topsy-turvy world and curled up in the corner. At last she knew what she must do. Tomorrow would come soon, then she would thank the kind gentleman and go back to the station, or—or— She fell asleep only half decided.

She slept so soundly that she hardly heard the door opening late in the morning. But gradually she opened her eyes and looked up. A pleasant, round-faced young Chinese woman stood in the doorway smiling. She wore a white jacket and padded dark-blue trousers. Her hair, slick and smooth as black satin and cut along the forehead and temples, showed that she was not a young girl, but a married woman.

She came over to the corner where Su-lan had been sleeping and squatted down beside her.

"Are you Su-lan?" she asked in a friendly low voice. "I am Dah Tai Tai. I've come to be with you today. We're going to do a lot of interesting things. But come now, first I'll help you wash up. Then we'll go down and eat breakfast. The *Hsien Sheng* has left for his work, but he will be back before noon."

Dah Tai Tai chatted away as if she had known Su-lan for years. All the while she talked, she kept busy doing things as if this was something that happened every day. She took Su-lan into the bathroom and turned on the water in the big white tub.

"You'll like this," she said. "It feels so good to get into a tub of warm water and scrub up."

Su-lan could hardly believe what she saw. Buckets and buckets of hot water! She remembered the hundreds of buckets of icy water she had carried home from the public well on the street, and how precious every drop of that water was. But here the water continued to run, and the steam arose in clouds.

Dah Tai Tai kept dipping her hand in the water. "You feel it," she said at last. "See if it is hot enough."

Su-lan had been privately fearing that she would scald to death if she got into it, but when she put her hand in it, it felt just right.

All the while the water had been running, Dah Tai Tai had been unfastening the clasps on Su-lan's jacket and helping her undress as if this were the most natural thing in the world to do. Su-lan decided to make believe that this *was* the most natural thing in the world to do, although she had never before in all her life taken an "all-over" bath.

How wonderful it felt! She loved the fragrant soap that Dah Tai Tai handed her. The only soap she had used before coming here had been strong and coarse.

Dah Tai Tai helped her dry off. "Kuei-bin said he thought you had been on a long trip or something, and didn't bring any extra clothes, so I brought these over." She left Su-lan with the towel draped around her, and brought from the closet a fresh white cotton jacket, a new pair of pale-blue cotton trousers, and finally a slim blue gown. "These used to belong to my sister when she was about your age, and I think they will just about fit you."

"There's a mirror in the other room," Dah Tai Tai said while Su-lan pulled the blue gown over her head. "Come, now, and you can see how you look. Would you like me to help you with your hair? It is so long and thick."

Su-lan tried not to show her excitement. When she looked at her reflection in the mirror, she wanted to pinch herself to make sure that this was not a dream. The clothes were the prettiest she had ever worn.

Dah Tai Tai chatted on as she led the way to the kitchen. There Su-lan ate the rice and *ts'ai* Kuei-bin had prepared. While she ate, Dah Tai Tai and Kuei-bin chatted like old friends. They laughed and joked a great deal. At last Su-lan was convinced that they were brother and sister.

When Stanley Brown returned from his office at lunchtime, Kuei-bin, Dah Tai Tai, and Su-lan were still in the kitchen.

"I thought I'd find you here," he said. "But, who is this?" he exclaimed as he stared at Su-lan. "Stand up and let me look at you! My, how fine you look!"

Su-lan did indeed look very different, and the long *kua-tzu* instead of the short jacket made her look older and slimmer.

"Have you been out to see the garden?" he asked. "Come with me; I want to show you my garden, and then I have some things I want to talk about."

Su-lan had never seen such a beautiful garden. She followed Mr. Brown as he led her along the paths and pointed out some of his favorite flowers.

"Sit down," he said, pointing to a stone bench. "What are we going to do with you? I can't keep you here, you know."

"Yes, I know." Su-lan's voice had a note of sadness in it.

"There's nothing for you to do here, of course, and you wouldn't be happy all by yourself. Have you ever been to school?"

"No, but Goh Tai Tai taught me to read. I've never had much time. I would love to go to school."

"Well, we'll figure it out someway so you can go to school. But you need a home first. What would you think about going back home?"

Su-lan hung her head. She fingered the material of her jacket. Then in a low sad voice she spoke.

"I once said I'd *never* go back. But although I do not feel that way now, I don't think it would be a help to them or to me to go back. And Fan Tai Tai might find out and make trouble for them or try to get me back."

"I think you are right. And we'll rule that out for now. Have you been thinking about this? What would you *like* to do, Su-lan?"

"All the time I was at Fan Tai Tai's I thought and thought. I planned and schemed what I could do if I could run away. I had many ideas. Maybe some family would hire me to help with the children or with the cooking. I know how to work. I like being busy. I'd like to go to school. Maybe sometime I could study to be a nurse—or maybe—"

"Good! But you're still just a little girl, and the thing you need most of all is a home where you can go to school and make up lost time. I'm beginning to think of an idea for you that might work out. We'll discuss it later."

The very next day Mr. Brown told Su-lan his plan. He returned in the middle of the morning and found her in the kitchen with

Kuei-bin and Dah Tai Tai again. Su-lan noticed a peculiar twinkle in his blue eyes, and an expression of being particularly pleased with himself. He had a bright package under his arm.

"Come into the other room, Su-lan. I've got some news for you. Really big, big news. But first here's a present for you." He handed Su-lan the package wrapped in colored paper and ribbon.

"For me?" She looked at it in amazement, but made no move to open it.

"Yes, it's for you. Aren't you going to open it?"

Su-lan carefully untied the ribbon and removed the paper. There were three colorful picture books with writing beside the pictures. But the writing was not anything she could read. Certainly these were not Chinese characters!

"I thought maybe you could learn some English while you are here," Mr. Brown continued. "It looks as if you will be needing it."

And then he told her that his sister, who lived in a big house in Shanghai, had consented to take Su-lan, for a while anyway. "She hasn't promised to keep you, mind; but she knows lots of people, and she will be looking for a home for you. She has four little girls already, so maybe it's too much for me to expect that she will take another one, especially—" he hesitated and then said, "especially someone she doesn't know at all. How does this sound to you, Su-lan? Would you like to go?" He hardly gave her time to answer, but went on, "You'll go by train to Tientsin and from there by boat to Shanghai. My sister will meet you there."

Arrival in Shanghai

The *Dairen Maru* sailed smoothly over the yellow waters of the Hwang Pu River as she moved toward the dock on the Bund in Shanghai. Su-lan pushed her way through the crowd of third-class passengers to the rail on the forepart of the lower deck.

River craft of all shapes and sizes bobbed about on the water—clumsy, creaking junks with brightly colored sails, warships from different nations of the world lying at anchor, as well as many other small steamers like the *Dairen Maru*. Tiny, salmon-colored sampans, flat-bottom boats propelled along by an oar from behind, skimmed in and out among the larger boats. Su-lan's eyes missed none of the wonderful sights.

She never could have believed that there were such magnificent buildings in the world as lined the waterfront for miles and miles; tall, tall buildings with towers reaching into the sky, and white colonnades shining in the sun. On the other side of the river wharves and piers and hundreds of luxurious houseboats moored in their private berths were ranged up and down the bank. Here and there a little spot of green, a park between the massive square buildings, showed up.

Su-lan could hardly believe this was all real and not a dream. The whole trip had been a thrilling and exciting experience. This riding high above the water on a big ship, Su-lan would never forget. But when she spoke of it to the other passengers, they laughed and said, "Why, the *Dairen Maru* is a dinky little tub, and we are counting the minutes until we can get off."

But not so with Su-lan, who had fortunately escaped seasickness, even while surrounded by dozens of unhappy travelers down in the women's cabin in the bowels of the boat. She hated to see the trip end. Now she had a sort of quivery feeling in her stomach as she thought of meeting the Morrisons. What if they didn't like her? Maybe they wouldn't be able to find a home for her. And what if they didn't? But she determined not to worry too much about it; for the moment she would enjoy letting her eyes wander from one curious sight to the next.

The ship pushed slowly along and finally docked at the wharf. The passengers surged onto the gangplank as soon as possible, but Su-lan did as Mr. Brown had instructed. She went back to the lounge and waited. It seemed that she waited a very long time. She began to wonder if maybe she would still be on the ship when it pulled out and went back to Tientsin. And then she saw the foreign lady in a brown suit come in the door.

The lady looked around the room. Seeing Su-lan, the only person in the room, she came over quickly.

"Are you Su-lan?" she asked in Chinese.

Su-lan noticed her eyes, deep blue like Stanley Brown's, smiling and friendly. Curly reddish-brown hair framed her face, and on one side of her head perched a tiny hat.

Su-lan stood up. "Yes, Tai Tai, I am Su-lan." For a moment they stood looking at each other, saying nothing. The hair with the touch of red in it did not seem so very peculiar to Su-lan as it would have a few months ago. And the likeness of this person to Stanley Brown gave her assurance in some intangible way.

"Did you have a bad trip? Are you very tired? Were you sea-sick?" The Shanghai dialect, different from the Pekingese, sounded strange. Su-lan could hardly understand most of the lady's words.

"Oh, no, I had a wonderful trip. I have never seen so much water. I liked it very much." She began to chatter about all the interesting things that had happened to her on the way.

"Do you have any baggage, anything else besides this?" Mrs. Morrison asked, pointing to the package Su-lan carried.

"No, that is all." Su-lan had brought her one possession, the shawl from home, neatly wrapped in a package. She carried under her arm the picture books Mr. Brown had bought her.

"Come along, then, we have a long ride ahead of us, and I know there are four little girls very anxious to see you."

As they reached the pier gates, scores of shouting blue-jacketed coolies rushed upon them as if to take them bodily and seat them in their rickshas. Behind them, ragged *mafoos* (drivers) were calling their prices, each insisting that a ride in his carriage would be cheaper than in anyone else's.

Mrs. Morrison waved them away with a brusque motion and a few words and piloted Su-lan through the crowd until she came to where two rickshas were waiting by themselves. There was no bargaining, and evidently these were private rickshas. Mrs. Morrison seated Su-lan in one and then stepped into the other and seated herself. The coolies shuffled off at a trot.

Su-lan, usually eager to take in all the sights and sounds, now sat back in the ricksha, preoccupied with other thoughts. Would the Morrisons like her? What would the little girls be like? What would become of her if— The thoughts tumbled through her mind.

"We are almost home." Mrs. Morrison broke into her thoughts.

There was no wall around the house, but a high hedge and a small gatehouse set at one side of a wide driveway. The ricksha runners turned in through a wide-open iron gateway. The gateman nodded and smiled as they passed. The coolies circled for a short distance along a gravel road winding between borders of flowering shrubs until they came to the steps of a large stone house with many windows and wide verandas.

"Well, here we are, Su-lan," Mrs. Morrison said as the coolies put down their shafts and she stepped down from her ricksha. She put out her hand to Su-lan. "Come on in and meet the girls."

Su-lan looked up at the house. As she looked at one of the windows, she thought she saw faces, but now, looking again, she saw only the curtained window.

Together they walked up the steps. Mrs. Morrison opened the door and ushered Su-lan in. She stopped as if glued to the spot.

So many people all looking at her at once! For just a moment it seemed that she saw only a crowd of solemn, staring faces. Then everyone began to talk and laugh. Su-lan stared at one and then another. If only she could understand what they said.

"Quiet, girls, calm down. I want you each to meet Su-lan." Mrs. Morrison raised her hand for silence. "First, there is Patricia. She is thirteen. Su-lan, this is Patricia."

"How do you do?" Patricia said, a slight frown puckering her brow, then remembered that Su-lan did not understand English.

"Hello!" said Su-lan, smiling. This one does not look too happy, Su-lan thought to herself. She does not smile.

"Hello! Hello! Hello!" shouted the other three girls at once. "Why, Mother, she speaks English. You didn't tell us she speaks English." And they started jabbering away to Su-lan.

"How old are you?" "Did you like the boat trip?" "Where did you learn English?"

Su-lan shook her head. Then she said to Mrs. Morrison in Chinese, "I learn one word on boat, Hello!"

And then Su-lan met in turn, Mary Jane, freckled and friendly, about her own age, with long brown braids of hair; seven-year-old Betty; and Connie, four. Behind the girls stood a tall, severe-looking Englishwoman.

"This is Miss Myrenda Austen, the girls' governess and teacher," Mrs. Morrison said. Then she took her to meet Tang Amah, small and wiry, in spotless white jacket and blue cotton trousers, who hovered over little Connie.

"I don't know how we can have any fun," Patricia complained in an aside to her mother after the introductions. "She can't talk English. But then, she probably won't be here very long. You're going to find another place for her, aren't you, Mother?"

"I can't answer that yet, but whether she remains with us or not I suggest that you never say anything even in English that you would not wish her to understand. She may not speak English now, but my guess is that she will be quick to learn and will surprise you."

"I can think of a lot of things to do that will be fun, and we won't have to talk English, either," Mary Jane said. "Well, not very much, anyway. We could play badminton or croquet and—"

"I can show her my kittens and bunny," Betty hurried to add.

"Me too. I wanna go too," Connie said.

"Mother, may I show Su-lan to her room?" Mary Jane asked a bit possessively. "And then maybe she can help me with my thousand-piece jigsaw puzzle. Do you think she's ever seen one?"

"Oh, let's all go along and see how she likes her room." Patricia weakened a little and did not want to be left out. And off they all went laughing and chattering like magpies.

Clouds on the Horizon

Any idea of finding another home for Su-lan disappeared after her first week at the Morrisons. Even Patricia ceased to remind her mother that the promise to Uncle Stanley had been for a temporary arrangement only. It was not that Su-lan immediately became one of them, but on the contrary, her very difference added much to the excitement of life. Many things that the family took for granted or things that had become commonplace now had a new meaning as the family saw them through Su-lan's eyes.

"That girl has a great capacity for wonder and enjoyment," Mr. Morrison said. "Her response is fun to watch."

The four girls thought so too. They took pleasure in showing Su-lan the wonders of the house and garden. How Su-lan wished she could tell Peony and Wang Shih Fu about the refrigerator with its magic ice cubes; the lights that turned on and off, and the beautiful lampshades; the bathrooms with their gleaming fixtures and silvery sprays of water right out of the wall; the sewing machine; the vacuum cleaner! To say nothing of the piano and the car.

Su-lan started classes with Betty and Mary Jane under Miss Austen's stern eyes. Patricia attended school in the International Settlement. At first Miss Austen regarded Su-lan as an intruder; but she soon had to admit, though grudgingly, that the girl had unusual powers of learning and adjustment.

The language barrier could not long hold out against the need for instant communication. The girls had so many things to show and tell Su-lan, and so many things they wanted to ask her.

"What did Fan Tai Tai look like?"

"What did she do to you that made you want to run away?"

"How did you happen to talk to Uncle Stanley at the railroad station?" They had heard just enough from Uncle Stanley to excite their curiosity.

Su-lan learned quickly. Soon her most common phrases were "What you call this?" and "How you say?" But there were so many things she wanted to know besides the names of things. Why did they all bow their heads at the table before eating, and who was the *Hsien Sheng* talking to then? She never could quite understand the words. Su-lan participated in the daily life of the family and tried to do what was expected of her, even if she did not always understand. She really enjoyed the times they sang together. This was pleasant even if she could not understand the words. The melodies sounded strange and a bit sad to her, compared to the five-tone musical scale of the Chinese and the high falsetto tones of the boatmen on the moat. She learned some of the words of the songs without knowing what they meant. Someday she would find out their meaning. One song she particularly liked. It had a catchy melody with a chorus, "His eye is on the sparrow, and I know He watches me." Su-lan sang this song with gusto.

Sometimes her energy and initiative got her into trouble. Once she decided to improve the arrangement of the living room furniture. It had always bothered her to see the casual position of the chairs and stands. She remembered how beautiful Fan Tai Tai's apartment was, with all the chairs straight with the wall, the cool elegance.

"What on earth are you doing, Su-lan?" Mrs. Morrison exclaimed, coming into the room before the job was finished and finding everything in a surprising state of disarray with Su-lan heaving and pushing on one of the large overstuffed chairs.

"Oh, I fix 'em real pretty like Chinese. Like Fan Tai Tai's, you know. Straight, like this," and she gestured effectively with her hands. But she could see at once that her plan did not meet with approval from the Tai Tai.

"You no like? Then I put back."

Mrs. Morrison smiled. She did not punish the child, and Su-lan soon realized that here no blows would fall on her head nor would there be slaps on her face. In this home she began to feel something she had never known before, love and understanding.

On another occasion a package had arrived in the mail for Mrs. Morrison, and Su-lan opened it without waiting for the lady to have this opportunity. In it were some sprays of cotton in the boll which some friend from America had sent for a floral arrangement. Su-lan had never seen cotton; but she had been hearing about it in school, and also about a man who had invented a machine to take out the seeds. She felt the flowery puffs and found the seeds, sure enough. She thought, "Oh, these seeds must come out. I'll surprise the Tai Tai and have it all ready."

When Mrs. Morrison arrived to see her present, she found the cotton nicely deseeded and in a little pile by itself and the seeds in a separate pile. Su-lan would never forget the look of disappointment that appeared on the Tai Tai's face when she saw what Su-lan had done.

"But you've spoiled it," Mrs. Morrison told her.

"I help you." Su-lan tried to show her repentance. But she learned a lesson that she never forgot about opening other people's mail.

As the days passed, Su-lan seemed to fill a special place in the life of each member of the household. She made fascinating toys of folded paper for Connie; she told stories to Betty, as soon as her language was adequate for the simplest story; she played outdoor games with Mary Jane and Patricia, and Patricia discovered a surprising bond between them in Su-lan's taste for pretty clothes.

"It's amazing the taste that girl has for clothes," Patricia told her mother. "She always knows the right colors and combinations and has an instinctive eye for line. And the way she loves rich fabrics! You'd think she came from the home of some aristocrat or from a home of wealth." Su-lan had been persuaded to wear Western clothes to please the Morrisons, but privately she had made up her mind that when she grew up she would always wear Chinese styles. She still wore her hair long, but sometimes loosened the braid and let it flow over her shoulders and down her back.

Mr. Morrison had his own special reasons for predicting some kind of career for Su-lan. He observed her personality and ways, and he had taken a special fancy to her because she was so genuine and unaffected and blunt in her speech. "That girl will make a good nurse, a teacher—or perhaps a general in the army," he said, laughing. He liked to tell the story of the time when most of the family were out of the house and he and Su-lan were home alone. He planned to do some dirty work in the yard and odd jobs around the house and had put on an old brown shirt that he liked for dirty jobs.

His wife had been telling him for a long time to get rid of the shirt, but he always retorted that he liked it since it was comfortable. That day Su-lan looked at him and said, "Mr. Morrison, you take off that shirt. I fix him. I sew him. I wash him. Not look good for *Hsien Sheng* wear shirt like that." And she really meant it! He had a hard time to convince her that he did not intend to take off that shirt.

Gradually the time came when Su-lan could tell them all they wanted to know about her life outside the wall, her months at the Lantern Shop, about Fan Tai Tai and Wang Shih Fu and Hu, and Goh Amah. She could even tell some of the Chinese stories that she told to Ming-li and the little sisters and brother on the *k'ang* at home. When she discovered the shock value of her stories, she enjoyed scandalizing her amazed audience with remarks such as, "You like eat little lambs? That's nothing. I use't' eat rats sometimes." And then she would burst into a loud laugh at the look of horror on their faces.

Betty especially liked to hear the "Story of the Seven Sisters," but the older girls were more interested in her account of her adventures in getting away from the Lantern Shop and Fan Tai Tai. One day after she had told this story, Mrs. Morrison, who had been knitting, remarked, "Su-lan, we can see, and I think you can too, that God has been watching over you, and has brought you to us."

Su-lan's eyes opened wide in surprise. "Who, me? You mean, *T'ien Fu* [heavenly Father] know me?"

"Of course. He knows each one of us."

"But so many people, so many Chinese people, so many white people, so many black people, so many. How can He—"

Here Mary Jane broke in. "You know, Su-lan, like we sing, 'His eye is on the sparrow, and I know He watches me!' "

"Oh, that what it mean?"

"Yes, and He not only watches you, but He has a plan for your life. All these things that have happened to you—there must be some purpose in the way they are working out," Mrs. Morrison added.

Su-lan pondered this thought.

On another occasion when she was talking about the old life and how much she liked Goh Amah, she spoke out with a flush of anger and hate, "I like Goh Amah, but I hate Fan Tai Tai!"

Mary Jane looked up. "Oh my! Su-lan, you mustn't hate Fan Tai Tai."

"Why not? She mean to me. She beat me. She very bad woman. Everyone hate Fan Tai Tai. They call her 'The Tiger'!"

"But that's past now. You must forgive her."

"Forgive? What that mean?"

"Well, it means that you must forget about the bad things she did to you and try to think kindly of her. Mother," Mary Jane said, turning to Mrs. Morrison, "how can I explain to Su-lan what it means for forgive?"

"Come here, Su-lan." Mrs. Morrison patted the stool beside her. "Sit close to me on this stool, and I will tell you a story, a true story that will show you what it means to forgive. You girls know this story, but I'd like you to listen too."

And so she told the old, old story, the story of Jesus, the best story in all the world to illustrate the meaning of love and forgiveness. And then she added, "You know, when we kneel down to pray and repeat, 'Forgive us our debts as we forgive our debtors,' it means that our *T'ien Fu,* our heavenly Father, asks us to forgive other people the same as He has forgiven us. You have heard us say the words and have been learning to say them with us. Now you can begin to understand the meaning and say them with your heart. This will be the most important lesson you will ever learn, Su-lan."

Before a year had passed, Su-lan seemed to be part of the Morrison family. There had never been any question in Mary Jane's mind but that her parents would legally adopt the Chinese girl. She loved Su-lan like a sister, and she knew that the rest of the family were fond of her too. But when Mr. Morrison talked to Su-lan about adoption, Su-lan shook her head. "Wait," she said.

"But why, Su-lan?" Mary Jane asked. "Why? To us you are like one of the family. We want you to be really truly one of the family. What's wrong? Maybe sometime we may go to America and would want to take you with us. Don't you like us?"

"Course I like. But—" Su-lan hesitated.

"But what?" Mary Jane pursued relentlessly.

"But I—but I Chinese."

"Well, so what? What difference does that make?"

"Make difference."

How could Su-lan explain what even she herself could hardly understand? But at times she had a strange feeling of being alone, of not quite belonging. How could they understand the flood of remembrances that often filled her mind? How could she forget the dark little room with all its discomforts and the family who were so often hungry? What were they doing now, Ming-li, Little Six, Mother, and all the others? Were they hungry or possibly sick? If there were only some way to help them. It did not seem right for her to have all the fine things she enjoyed and not be able to share with them. Maybe someday when she was a nurse or—

And then she thought of springtime in Peking, the oleanders and peonies, the pleasure barges on the moat, the feathery green veil that seemed to spread over the city as the days warmed and lengthened.

"I like to stay Chinese," was the best that Su-lan could think of at this time.

When she had been at Fan Tai Tai's, she had been one of the servants and had enjoyed their friendship and association—the jokes and fun, the sharing of hardships. But in the Morrison household she felt cut off from her own people and language and customs. The servants seemed to resent Su-lan. She could understand them far better than the Morrisons did, and could see through their little wiles and schemes. They no longer felt free to chatter away so carelessly among themselves when Su-lan was around. And she quickly sensed how they felt about her.

It had been worse since the time she had questioned Ho Shih Fu about twenty dollars' worth of soap used in one month. But, twenty dollars' worth of soap a month! What family could use that much soap? And yet, Mrs. Morrison would have paid it right along with the other bills if Su-lan had not spoken up. She had come into the kitchen when Ho was beginning to settle the accounts with Mrs.

Morrison. He had a sheaf of thin papers in his hand, all written in flowing Chinese script. The Tai Tai jotted down the figures as he went along, not really paying much attention. When Su-lan exclaimed about the twenty dollars for soap, Ho quickly corrected it, and they went on. Evidently Mrs. Morrison would not have questioned the amount, Su-lan decided. But Ho Shih Fu had not forgiven her.

Su-lan thought about these things. Ever since coming to Shanghai she had been conscious of a restlessness among the servants. They seemed to resent the foreigners. But Tang Amah was loyal, of that Su-lan felt sure. Ho Shih Fu and his helper, Ming, put on polite and smiling faces, but something smoldered underneath. And Su-lan knew that the Morrisons were utterly blind not only to the petty pilferings and small deceptions but to the unrest and antiforeign feelings that were spreading.

One evening Mrs. Morrison sent Su-lan with a message to Amah. As she walked through the servants' quarters, she noticed the door to the cook's room half open. From the room came the sound of excited voices all talking at once. Su-lan flattened herself against the wall and listened.

"I tell you," an unknown voice said, "anyone who is connected with those dog-nosed foreigners from now on is in for trouble. As soon as the thing breaks, they will be killed like pigs. It is only a matter of days."

Su-lan put her hand over her heart. Surely its pounding would reveal her presence. Should she go on to the Amah or go back to the Morrisons? Would those in the room see her if she walked past the open door? What was the meaning of such talk? Who was this strange visitor?

While she hesitated, the talking went on. Much of it she could not understand. But she heard Ming's voice, full of anger and hate, so different from the usual polite words he used in the presence of the Morrisons.

Su-lan decided that the messages to Amah could wait, and that she should not pass the doorway where she would be seen, but go back as quietly as possible. But before she could turn to leave, the visitor spoke again. In a harsh and commanding voice he told Ming and Ho to be at a party meeting tomorrow in the native city and to wear their red armbands. Su-lan wondered what kind of party that would be.

But she had heard enough. She left the servants' quarters and hurried back to the big house. She would tell the Morrisons at once what she had learned. But when she found Mrs. Morrison dressing to go out, Su-lan decided that this was not the time for the kind of news she had to tell.

And then, was it really true? Could it be only idle talk? she wondered. But the voices had certainly sounded most terribly serious. Why, from what they had been saying it sounded as if all the foreigners in China were in danger. She wanted to tell Mary Jane too but decided she should wait. Maybe she could find out some more and be more sure.

After she had gone to bed that night a scheme began to form. The next day Patricia and Mary Jane had dentist appointments. Miss Austen would go with them. While Betty and Connie, the younger girls, took their naps Su-lan would slip out and walk to the Chinese City and mix with the Chinese on the street. She would listen and read and see what she could find out. A tingle of excitement ran through her as she thought of her daring scheme.

She would dress in her Chinese clothes. No one would pay the slightest attention to her then. It would be fun to mix with the Chinese, smell the food cooking along the street, hear the familiar chatter of Chinese tongues, see the thousand and one familiar street activities so different from the ordinary city street. Of course she would have to get back before being missed so that no one would worry about her. Of course she could take care of herself. Hadn't she practically grown up on the street?

For a long time she lay awake thinking. Then she turned on her side and closed her eyes. Yes, tomorrow she would dress in her Chinese clothes and venture out. Perhaps she would find the talk in the servants' quarters had been but idle talk. If not—what would become of the Morrisons?

Su-lan's Mysterious Errand

The next day Su-lan slipped out of the driveway of the Morrison home and began her long walk to the Chinese City.

At first it seemed good to be out on the street, walking along like one of her people. She had put on the common blue suit that Dah Tai Tai had dressed her in that day at Stanley Brown's now over a year ago. It was getting a bit small, for she had grown rapidly; but because of its loose and roomy fit she could still wear it. It was fun to be in Chinese clothes again.

It seemed a very long time since those days in Peking; so much had happened. Not only on the outside—her dress, food, and pattern of life—but on the inside as well. What would she do with her life? Did God really have a purpose for her? The Morrisons had talked about it a great deal. But just now she must think of where she was going.

People and traffic of all kinds milled about on the street. Cars and buses had to make their way among the slower traffic of pedicabs and bicycles. Electric trams screeched their way down the center of the street. Swarms of pedestrians sauntered along the sidewalks or waited at street corners for transportation.

Su-lan walked along rapidly with a glow of excitement in being part of all the throbbing life about her. Most of the people were Chinese, but many foreigners rode past in rickshas or automobiles or in leisurely paced horse-drawn carriages. At some of the intersections tall turbaned Indian Sikhs, the policemen of Shanghai, directed traffic. These black-beared men from another country fascinated Su-lan. She had never seen such men until she had come to Shanghai.

Everything looked so normal now, so commonplace, so like every other time she had been along here with the family, sometimes in rickshas, sometimes in the car. Surely the words she had heard from the passageway the evening before were but hasty words resulting from some personal grudge or grievance. Certainly nothing to upset a whole city.

Bubbling Well Road after some distance became Nanking Road. Then Su-lan turned onto Thibet Road which led toward the Chinese City. She had gone with the Morrisons in the car a few times, and had seen the narrow streets filled with colorful shops selling brocades, jewelry, porcelain, and groceries. Often she had wished she could get out and walk along the little side streets. This part of Shanghai reminded her of the part of Peking outside the city wall where the Lantern Shop had been located.

Soon after leaving the side streets and fine houses of the foreigners she came into a section where numerous small shops lined the narrow streets. Su-lan idled along now, looking at the windows and watching the people. For a while she almost forgot her errand and the passage of time. Then, coming to a place where a crowd of people gathered around the entrance of a large store, she pushed her way to a position where she could see a large bulletin board posted beside a Chinese pharmacy. Several large posters showed fat, pompous, ugly men with huge bags of money driving small helpless coolies to work or pushing them into the mud with their big feet. Some of the ugly men had whips or bayonets in their hands. Su-lan knew at once by their large noses and foreign dress that the ugly men represented the foreigners in China. Across the top of the posters in giant-sized Chinese characters in bright red paint, the words stood out: "Drive out the dog-nosed foreigners. Get rid of foreign capitalists. Imperialists."

Su-lan turned to look at the faces of the people around her— well-dressed students, businessmen, and many older people who obviously could not read, for they were asking the others the meaning of the words. The answers and the talk showed anger and hate and not a word of defense for the foreigners.

The feeling of happy belonging Su-lan had enjoyed while walking down Bubbling Well Road left, and a great fear came over her. She felt as if these people could see inside her and know she was not one of them. She had to go, to get away fast, but just then she saw people hurrying down the street and gathering in a big mob on the next corner. As if compelled, Su-lan followed the crowd.

Before she knew it, she had been swallowed up by the crowd. Now she could not turn back if she wanted to. On every side the people wedged her in. For some time Su-lan could not see or hear anything but the people around her.

And then, as the crowd swayed this way and that, she finally caught a glimpse of some young men standing on a platform on top of a car decorated with pictures of foreigners, something like she had seen on the bulletin board. One young man shrieked in a sort of frenzy as he denounced all Americans and Britishers and foreigners in general. He told how they robbed the people and got control of all the land, and how their doctors cut people up and took out the eyes of little children. On and on he shouted until Su-lan thought he must faint with exhaustion.

Su-lan had heard enough now. She had to get back home and warn the Morrisons! Obviously they did not know about all this and that their own servants had plotted against them. It was important not to waste any time.

Gradually Su-lan extricated herself from the crowd; and, once out on the fringe, she turned quickly and started to walk rapidly toward Nanking Road and home.

"I will tell them right away," she resolved, "no matter if Ho should find out."

It was a long, long way home. Much longer it seemed than when she had come in the morning. Su-lan had plenty of time to think. This feeling of hate seemed all wrong. In Peking she had never seen or heard of such an attitude toward the foreigners. There the Americans and the British had been respected in spite of their peculiar looks and customs. "There must be lots and lots of Chinese who do not hate the foreigners," Su-lan thought. "Why, Mr. Stanley Brown and the Morrisons do not hate." Su-lan thought of all that they had done for her. The four Morrison girls were closer to her than her own sisters. She wondered now if she had been away from the house long enough to be missed. She had not planned to be away so long.

She had been missed by Mary Jane and Patricia. The long trip to town by ricksha had been tiresome; and as soon as they returned, they dashed into the house to find Su-lan for a game of badminton.

She was not in the living room. Patricia dashed upstairs to look in the bedrooms. She found Betty and Connie busy with paper dolls.

"Have you seen Su-lan?" Patricia asked.

The little girls shook their heads.

"She's not up here," Pat reported to Mary Jane.

"Well, where on earth can she be?" Mary Jane asked. "I've been out in the kitchen. There's no one out there, not even Ming or Ho. Maybe she's hiding somewhere to tease us."

"OK, then, where would she hide?" They made a thorough search of the closets, outside in the garden, and even the storeroom on the third floor. But not a sign of Su-lan.

Finally, when they had exhausted all their ideas and had looked everywhere they could think of, they stood at the living-room window and watched for their mother to come home. Mother would probably know. She could always solve their problems.

It seemed hours before they saw her coming up to the door, and then she looked so worried that they were sure something dreadful must have happened to Su-lan. They pounced on her at once.

"Mother, oh, Mother, do you know where Su-lan is?"

"Why, no. She must be around somewhere," Mrs. Morrison said without seeming to be concerned at all. "Now, girls, don't bother me right now. I must call your father about something very important." She put her hat and bag on the stand and hurried into the study and closed the door.

"She didn't even seem to care about Su-lan," Patricia said.

"Why, I don't think she even heard what we said," Mary Jane stated, shaking her head sadly.

The girls walked over to the door that their mother had closed behind her. They tried to listen. They heard Mother give the operator their father's office number.

"Must be something real important," Patricia said. "She hardly ever calls Daddy at the office."

"Sh-sh!" Mary Jane motioned as they heard Mother's voice ask for Mr. Morrison. The girls looked at each other.

"Something must be troubling Mother," Patricia said.

After a while Mrs. Morrison came out of the study.

"Mamma, Su-lan is gone!" Patricia exclaimed again. "She is really gone! We can't find her anywhere! Where can she be?"

"Oh, she *must* be around somewhere," Mrs. Morrison assured them. "Don't get so excited. Why, of course she must be here. Where else could she be?"

"But she isn't. Really, Mother. We've looked and looked and no one knows anything about her. She was not here when we came back from the dentist. You don't think she would run away, do you?" Mary Jane asked anxiously.

"She did run away from Fan Tai Tai, you know," reminded Patricia.

"Oh, of course she wouldn't run away. We've been good to her, and she couldn't possibly have any reason to run away. I'm sure she'll come in soon. Maybe she's out at the servants' quarters. Did you look there?"

The girls noticed the worry lines on their mother's forehead. What they did not know was the news she had heard at the club that afternoon. All the women had been talking about the war that had been menacing other parts of the country. But Shanghai, with its International Settlement, had always escaped. But now it seemed that it *was* coming to Shanghai. Any day the consul might order the women and children to leave. They might have to board the warships for safety for a few weeks, or even flee to Tsingtao for several months.

Then they all heard a car in the driveway, and Mr. Morrison came into the house. He did not seem worried, the girls thought. But where was Su-lan?

Mrs. Morrison, with a rush of words, repeated to her husband what she had heard at the club. Then she added, "And Su-lan is not here. She must have gone out somewhere while we were away this afternoon, but we can't think of any reason why she should go anywhere by herself. I am very cross at her for causing us any trouble right at this time." She stopped speaking as Miss Austen came into the room.

"Well, you know that girl was just a common little brat until she came here, and there's no telling what she might be up to," Miss Austen said.

"Don't worry about her," Mr. Morrison laughed. "Anyone who

could survive the troubles that girl has had and come out smiling is all right. I am sure there is some good explanation. She will turn up and be all right. Come on, let's eat. I'm hungry." He seemed not at all perturbed by the news.

They sat down at the table, but the girls couldn't help worrying about Su-lan. Every time they tried to speak to their Mother she seemed preoccupied, while Mr. Morrison seemed only eager to eat the tasty food that had been prepared for the family. The girls spoke in low tones to each other. What would they do if Su-lan didn't come back that night? Where would they go to search for her? And worst of all, what if she didn't *want* to come back?

Something Important to Tell

But Su-lan did want to get back. She had walked for what seemed miles. It hadn't seemed so far earlier when she had left the big house and walked to the Chinese City. But now she was hungry and thirsty. The sun set, and darkness began to settle over the city. Supper would be finished at the Morrison home. This did not concern her except that she realized that she would be missed and the Morrisons would be worried about her. Maybe they wouldn't understand her leaving without telling them where she was going. However, she now had something important to tell them, something they should know. She quickened her steps.

When at last she reached the iron gate, she found it still open. The big light by the street had been left on as if there were company. Who could it be? She rushed past the gatehouse hoping the gateman would not see her. Then she noticed all the lights on downstairs in the big house. Probably the *Hsien Sheng* and Tai Tai (she had never been able to call them Mother and Dad as they wanted her to) were still in the big living room. The windows upstairs were dark, and she wondered if the girls were asleep. She walked rapidly along the gravel driveway and up the steps to the front door. How would they treat her? She did not feel very happy about what she had done.

The door opened easily at Su-lan's touch. She saw Mr. and Mrs. Morrison in the living room. They seemed to be talking very seriously as she entered. Then their voices broke off as Mrs. Morrison looked up and saw her. Quickly she jumped up and ran to Su-lan, putting her arms around her.

"Su-lan, my dear child, where have you been? We have been

114

so worried! Oh, we're so glad you are safely home again. You must be hungry. Come, let me get you something to eat."

Mr. Morrison smiled from his chair at the table. Su-lan smiled back. It seemed that Mr. Morrison hadn't been in the least worried, and that he knew there were times when anyone liked to go away without making any explanations. But she turned quickly to Mrs. Morrison.

"Oh, Tai Tai, I am so sorry. I did not plan to be gone so long, it's just that I— Well, the other day I heard something—"

At this point Mary Jane's voice called from upstairs.

"Is that Su-lan?"

"Yes, she's back now," Mrs. Morrison answered.

"Su-lan's back! Su-lan's back!" Mary Jane shouted. And suddenly all four girls in their pajamas came running downstairs and into the living room. They hugged and squeezed Su-lan and asked all kinds of questions.

"Where have you been?"

"Why didn't you tell us?"

"We've been looking everywhere for you."

"What are you wearing those clothes for?"

Su-lan motioned for them to be quiet. "I have something very important to tell you. I heard something the other day. I wanted to find out if it was true. It is very important. You must listen."

But Mrs. Morrison shooed the four girls off to bed.

"Come, girls, back to bed now," she said. "I'm going to get Su-lan some supper and then she's going to bed. You can talk to her in the morning." Then turning to Su-lan, she said, "In the morning you can tell us all about it. But not tonight."

Reluctantly Su-lan put off the telling of her news until the next day. Some time later when she lay in her own comfortable bed, she pondered the strange ways of the foreigners. Her family had never been given to hugging and kissing and showing affection. Oh, yes, they cuddled and kissed Little Six. But here affection bubbled over all the time. Not being accustomed to it, Su-lan always put up a wall of coolness and drew away. But this welcome home she enjoyed. But why hadn't she been able to make them listen to her news? For some time Su-lan lay on her back thinking these thoughts. Then she heard a slight rustle at the door.

"Su-lan, are you awake?"

"Yes, is that you, Mary Jane?"

"May I come in with you for a while? I can't sleep. Oh, Su-lan, I—I was so worried about you. We hunted and hunted, and we couldn't understand why you had gone away without telling us. Where did you go, Su-lan? *Why* didn't you tell us?" Mary Jane asked as she slid into bed beside Su-lan without waiting for an answer.

"I didn't intend to be gone so long, truly, Mary Jane. I had to find out something—something very important. I wanted to tell your mother, but she wouldn't let me."

"I think Mother thought you were going to explain and apologize, and she was so glad you were back that she didn't care why you went away. And besides, Mother has had something else on her mind today. I know she is worried about something, but I don't really know what it is. But tell me what you learned. I'm just dying to know."

Su-lan repeated the words she had heard outside Ming's door and told what she had seen in the Chinese City. "Your mother should know about this. She doesn't dream of how things are."

"That's terrible," Mary Jane gasped. "Did they actually talk about killing? We've got to tell Mother. First thing in the morning we'll go together. But we must be careful not to let Ming or Ho Shih Fu hear. That would be bad for all of us, and especially you." Mary Jane spoke in a whisper. "Do you suppose Mother knows? Maybe that's why she seemed so worried about something she heard at the club today."

And at that very moment Mrs. Morrison turned to her husband and asked, "Do you really think things are as bad as the ladies at the club seem to think? I'm having a few ladies in on Thursday, and I hope this won't frighten my guests away."

Bob snorted. "My dear, I have been afraid to alarm you, but maybe that is just what you need. I believe that this time Shanghai is in for a real shooting war. You'd better begin to think about packing up. You and the children might have to leave very suddenly—"

"Well, I'm not going to get alarmed! You know how often we hear these things. Why, I've heard this story every year since I came to China. Everyone gets excited and frightened, and rumors go around. The soldiers are right at the outskirts of the city and all that, and we must rush to the mountains or the beach. Then after a few weeks it blows over. We get a new government, and life goes on as before. I'm not going to get scared out of here now."

Mrs. Morrison sat at the dressing table putting her hair up in pin curls. She made a grimace at her husband's reflection in the mirror as he stood behind her.

"Well, of course, if that afternoon tea is the most important thing in the world, you probably would go ahead with it even if guns popped off all around you. Florence, I don't think you realize at all what this may mean. This is really different. A storm is just ready to break. Even before this present crisis, an antiforeign element has been growing like a smoldering volcano. All it will take will be some small incident to cause it to erupt into a wild frenzy of hate and violence. But come on to bed. Let's sleep now. We can talk in the morning."

His wife turned out the light and climbed into bed. "It's probably because I've never seen any war that I just can't seem to think there is anything real about this."

No Tea Party Today

The next morning gave promise of a hot day. The fragrance of honeysuckle and roses hung in the slightly humid air after recent rains.

As soon as Su-lan awoke, she remembered what she had tried to tell Mrs. Morrison the night before. She found Mary Jane already up and dressing and suggested that they go at once to tell the news.

"You come with me, and maybe she will have time to listen now," she said. Together they hurried downstairs. They found Mother in the kitchen talking to Ho and Ming.

Su-lan and Mary Jane thought she would never finish talking to cook about the pastries and cakes for the party and giving a lot of little details about the polishing of silver and preparing the tables.

Finally, as she finished, the girls besieged her.

"Mother, Su-lan has something important to tell you," Mary Jane began. "Remember, last night—"

Mrs. Morrison groaned. "I'm so busy right now, girls! I'm not worried about last night. Let's forget about yesterday." She smiled and gave each girl a light kiss. "Come, now, it's time to eat."

"But, Mother, this is really important. I think you should hear what Su-lan has to tell," persisted Mary Jane.

"Well, later, but not now. I've got a million things to think about today, getting ready for my party tomorrow. Sit down and eat your breakfast."

They sat down at the breakfast table, and Ho Shih Fu, smiling and proud as usual, brought pomelo or grapefruit or pineapple, then cooked cereal and toast and a choice of hot breads, muffins, scones, and popovers on a silver tray covered with a linen napkin.

Mr. Morrison had already gone to his city office. Miss Austen hardly ever appeared at breakfast but had a tray in her room. The older girls had little to say and did not seem very hungry. Betty and Connie were too involved with syrup and jam to do much talking. The amah stood by to help. In fact, Connie did hardly anything without Amah right beside her. All her five years she had been pampered and waited on. All day Amah hovered near the child until night when she tucked her into bed.

Mary Jane and Su-lan could hardly help staring at Ho as he carried food in and empty plates out. Had the food been poisoned? The girls looked furtively at each other.

"Oh, dear," Mrs. Morrison spoke up. "I hope the tailor has the new dress ready that I plan to wear. I wonder if three dozen sand-wiches will be enough. Let's see, what new and unusual thing could I add to the *hors d'oeuvres*? I've got a thousand little details still to tell Ho." And with hardly a breath she rushed on, "The breakfast is unusually good, isn't it?" she asked no one in particular, and then went on. "They have their faults, but really I do have wonderful servants. I don't know what I would do without them."

The jangle of the telephone brought Patricia to her feet. "I'll get it, Mother." When she came back to the table she announced, "No school today for me. There is too much unrest in the city."

"Oh, good. You can help me then," her mother said, getting up and hurrying out to the greenhouse, Su-lan and Patricia follow-ing.

"The flower borders need some trimming before tomorrow to make a neat appearance," Mrs. Morrison said.

Ma, the garden boy, was not around, but Ho Shih Fu appeared, looking frightened and nervous. He wore a red armband, and had a letter in his hand.

"Please, missee, look see. Just now letter come from home in Honan. Must go home. Grandfather velly sick. Must go at once. Here, you see, you lead—" Ho pushed the letter into her hands.

"But, Ho, I have been counting on you for tomorrow, you know. Can't you wait? You can go the very next day. Really I just can't let you go today." She looked at the letter written in a fine faint Chinese script on tissue-thin rice paper.

"Oh, don't wolly, missee. I be back, few days. Two, thlee days,

I come back. You see." He eased the letter from her hands and turned back toward the house.

"Well," Mrs. Morrison exclaimed. "That old trick. Sick grandfather, indeed! I wonder if Bob could be right." She hurried back to the house.

Just then Mary Jane appeared at the door. "Mother, Daddy's on the phone."

Mrs. Morrison went into the study and lifted the receiver.

"Florence?" her husband's voice sounded tense. "I'll be home as soon as I can. Tell the girls to get ready to leave. You will have not more than half an hour to pick up the most necessary things. You won't be able to take much, not more than a suitcase apiece. Don't worry about anything else. The American consul has ordered all women and children to leave at once—"

"But, Bob—" Mrs. Morrison interrupted.

"Listen. I've been phoning all over the place to find out as much as I can. There is a gunboat anchored in the Hwang Pu due to sail tomorrow or next day. You must be on it. You can't risk staying another day."

"But this is impossible," Florence protested. "How can we possibly be ready to leave in half an hour? Is this really necessary? I don't see how—" She stuttered and stammered her objections.

"Get busy, Florence. Don't waste time. The report has come in of sad incidents in many places. In Nanking the Americans barely escaped with their lives. They had gathered at the consulate where they were surrounded by the Communists. A few sailors with guns were guarding the stairwell to the second floor, and when they saw that the situation was desperate one of them went up on the roof and signaled to the gunboats lying in harbor and they opened fire. With both the British and the American ships firing their guns a narrow corridor was made by which the foreigners could escape from the consulate. They had to be let down from the top of the city wall by a rope and finally were taken aboard the ship. Do I need say any more? I'll be there in half an hour. Have everyone ready."

Mrs. Morrison stood with the receiver in her hand after her husband had hung up.

"What's the matter, Mother?" Mary Jane asked, from the open door. "What has happened?"

"War, Mary Jane. It's really here now, and we have only half an hour to get together the most necessary things. We won't be able to take much, not more than a suitcase apiece." Mrs. Morrison put down the receiver and slumped into a chair.

"But, Mother, that's what Su-lan has been trying to tell you, about how all the foreigners are in danger—"

"I've been too blind to see. I thought it might not be too serious, that is, I hoped—" She brought herself up with a jerk. "But that is neither here nor there now. Your father will be here soon. We must be ready. There is a ship leaving for America and—"

Mary Jane let out a whoop. "America! America! Oh, just wait till I tell—"

"What's this about America?" Miss Austen asked, coming into the room, followed by Betty, Connie, and Amah.

"What did you say about America? Are we really going?" Betty asked.

"Let's not get excited!" Mother urged.

The girls began to chatter with Miss Austen and Amah. Mrs. Morrison watched her daughters' happy faces as they talked about going to America. Betty had been too small on their last visit to remember America; Connie had never been there, and so it would be the same as a first visit to both of them. Patricia and Mary Jane had very happy memories and looked forward to going to America again.

"Where's Su-lan?" Mrs. Morrison asked suddenly, looking around the room.

The girls stopped their chatter and looked around in surprise. "Why, I thought she was here! Su-lan will go with us, of course, won't she, Mother?" they all asked at once.

"Of course," Mrs. Morrison answered. "But where is the girl?"

They found her alone in the kitchen.

"What are you doing in here?" They looked around the usually well-ordered kitchen. Breakfast dishes, still unwashed, cluttered the counter and sink; milk bottles half full of milk still stood in the warm room; butter and left-over foods had not been put in the refrigerator.

"I came out to get a drink," Su-lan said, spreading her hands, "and this is what I found. Ming and Ho have gone. I went out to the servants' quarters, and they have all gone. Things are in a terrible mess out there too. I thought I would start cleaning up."

"Good girl! That's just like you. But never mind now. Go up to your room and pick out a few things that you will need most. A small suitcase. We are going to America. The consul has ordered us out, and you must come with us."

"You will, won't you?" Mary Jane begged.

"Yes, I will go." She smiled as she looked from one to the other. Then she added, "I'll hurry; get ready; help girls," she said, reverting back to broken English.

"That's fine. And now, everyone get busy. Hurry. Too much time has already passed." Mrs. Morrison clapped her hands, shooing the girls on their way. "Go up and pick out a few things, the things you will need most, like changes of clothes, sweaters, and toilet articles."

It seemed only a few minutes when the door opened and they heard Mr. Morrison's hearty voice calling out, "Everybody ready? All aboard!"

The family appeared from different rooms carrying their cases and a few things under their arms.

"What's going to happen to everything here?" Mrs. Morrison asked.

"I'll come back as soon as I get you safely deposited on a ship," Mr. Morrison stated. "I'll send what I can to America or store things away. Others up-country have lost everything they left behind, but I'll do the best I can. But come on, let's get moving."

He looked at Su-lan and smiled. "Su-lan, I'm glad to see that you are ready to go with us too. I don't think we could have budged Mary Jane without you."

"Oh, yes," she said, "I like very much to go. When I came here, I needed you very much. Now you go to America, no amah, no Ho Shih Fu. You need Su-lan very much. I help, I work—"

"Nonsense, Su-lan! My dear child, you are going to school in America. Later you can take nurses' training if you wish, or whatever you want. Then someday you can come back to China—the China you love. Perhaps someday we may all come back—" Mrs. Morrison sighed. "But there is no time for talking. Let's be on our way."

The girls rushed to the car. Only Su-lan looked back. There was a movement of the curtain at the living-room window and Su-lan felt sure she saw Amah's sad face for a moment. Would she ever see Amah or this pleasant house or China, her China, again?

"Why, oh, why did this have to happen?" Mrs. Morrison's voice brought Su-lan up with a start.

Su-lan slipped her small hand in Mrs. Morrison's. "Maybe like you say, Tai Tai," Su-lan answered softly, and a smile formed on her lips, "God have purpose. God have purpose for me; God have purpose for you."

DATE DUE

	DATE DUE		